BETWEEN TWO WORLDS

Between Two Worlds

BY SARAH SARGENT

Ticknor & Fields
Books for Young Readers
NEW YORK 1995

Published by Ticknor & Fields Books for Young Readers,
A Houghton Mifflin company, 215 Park Avenue South,
New York, New York 10003

Manufactured in the United States of America

Book design by David Saylor
The text of this book is set in 12-point Caslon 540.

BP 10 9 8 7 6 5 4 3 2 1

Library of Congress Cataloging-in-Publication Data
Sargent, Sarah.
Between Two Worlds / by Sarah Sargent.   p.   cm.
Summary: Bored by her ordinary life,
thirteen-year-old Janet imagines herself a character
on her favorite soap opera.
ISBN 0-395-66425-X
[1. Soap operas—Fiction.] I. Title.
PZ7.S2479Be 1995
[Fic]—dc20   93-24533   CIP   AC

For Dorothy Markinko

BETWEEN TWO WORLDS

Forest Grove

"I don't think it's fair." Jan rocked her Coke can back and forth, slopping a bit over the edge onto the white tabletop. The new house was blindingly white. Why did she have a wicked urge to pollute it? A smear of grape jelly on the kitchen tiles, perhaps. A splash of tomato juice on the ivory area rug. The temptation flashed through her mind so fast that Jan barely acknowledged it. She reached for a paper napkin and mopped up the spilled Coke.

Her mom frowned. "We all have to adjust, Jan. Don't think I haven't been through times like this— moving away from friends, needing to start over. What you have to do is to see it as a challenge." Karen McIver took a sip of coffee and sighed. "For instance, in five years, Jannie, you'll be leaving for college. Think about that. To *do* anything, *be* anybody, you have to make these kinds of breaks. You can't cling to the old neighborhood just because you're used to it."

"But I don't see why—" Jan's voice was rising.

"Janet, we've been over it, OK? You can't go for a month and stay with Monica at the lake because we need you here. With all the moving expenses, we don't want to pay for regular daycare for Josh. You're thirteen, old enough to be realistic and help out. And the bottom line is, I think it's what's best for you. You have to learn to live here, Jan. *Here. Here.* In Forest Grove, for heaven's sake. And most of the world would love to change places with you. That's what makes me mad."

"It's nice," Jan said grudgingly. "I never said it wasn't nice out here. But there's all rich kids out here. Snobs."

"It's not snobbery to want to associate with people who've made a success of their lives." Karen poured herself a swallow or two more decaf. "You'll fit in. It just takes a little time. I'm just not buying these arguments, Jan. You know I'm not. We've been through it."

"If I could stay with Monica at the lake, I could

kind of prepare myself. You know . . . do the reading list for my new class . . . like that."

Karen laughed and shook her head. "Well, you're getting creative, I've got to say that. You forget I know you, Jan. You? Pick up a reading list before August is half over?"

"There're fewer distractions out at the lake," Jan said stiffly. She hated being laughed at. When she had children she would never laugh at them. Not ever.

"Jan, you've got all day. All you've got to do is run a few loads of wash and look after Kevin. I'd love to see you showing initiative, reading the list, getting ahead. It's true middle school out here will be more competitive. You *should* get going if you're going to keep up."

Jan nodded numbly. She hated her mom. Never in a thousand years would her mother grasp what Jan was going through. Starting middle school was scary enough if you were going with friends. Jan's family had moved after school was out, to let her and Josh finish the semester in town. So how could she meet anybody? Jan tapped the side of her Coke can, thinking over her situation.

True, she did have two kind of semi-friends, Jess and Amy. That was because Jan's mom had gone behind her back and signed her up for tennis at the club. And then dropped Jan off wearing the wrong kind of shoes so she felt like an idiot. On the courts at the park in the old neighborhood, Monica and Jan had always worn the same running shoes they wore everyplace. But as soon as Jan walked up, the blond girl, Amy, had stared at her shoes. Jan had felt Amy's eyes and shifted from foot to foot. She'd looked around quickly. The others had lower shoes and, except for Jan, they were all wearing new ones. Tennis shoes. They'd all bought shoes just for the courts.

"Nice shoes," Amy had said, smirking sweetly. "You jog over?"

"Shut up, Amy," the girl with long brown hair had said. "I'm Jess. Did you move to Candlewick Lane a couple of weeks ago?" Jan had nodded. "I ride my bike past there, going to the mall. I saw you."

"Hi, I'm Jan," she'd said, her face burning. Jess was nice. But when somebody told a joke, the others looked at Amy to see how hard to laugh.

Amy had a great body and perfect features. Her nose was turned up just enough. Her hair looked like a shampoo commercial. And she was a great mimic.

Once during a break when Gunther, the pro, had gone inside to answer the phone, Amy had them all falling over laughing, with her imitation of his German accent and his habit of chewing on his lip when he served.

"De follow-true, det's all, geurls, de follow-true." Amy had mussed her hair forward and chewed her lip and puffed out her nostrils, and they'd howled. Jan had seen Jess looking uneasy when Gunther came from behind the tree. Jan squirmed, but something in her didn't care. Something in her hoped he had heard. Jan had felt put down too often in Forest Grove: Let somebody else be the victim for a change.

Back in the city, Jan reflected, her whole life hadn't been a contest. In Forest Grove, as soon as she'd met five or six kids that'd be in her class, Jan saw that they were all watching her and totting up points. Points for her hair, her clothes, her shoes, her jokes, her boobs, her earrings.

Jan bought some hair mousse and a jar of lash-extender gel. She noticed that Amy liked gummy bears and she kind of happened to always have some. But when Monica had called and asked if Jan could go out to the lake with Monica's family for the rest of the summer, Jan's eyes had filled with tears of relief. She had to wear her mom down, keep at her and keep at her. Make her see.

Across from Jan, Karen idly tapped the handle of her coffee spoon and gazed off into the distance, lost in her own reflections. Jan was annoyed all over again, seeing how quickly her mom had forgotten all about her daughter's misery.

"Why'd we come out here, then?" Jan narrowed her eyes. "If now we can't afford to do anything? Just so we can live in a big house in the suburbs? What's wrong with where we were?"

"The big house, the nice area—those are just the externals, Jan. It's complicated. Dad and I wanted a change." Karen ran her hand through her frosted blond hair. "You aren't a child, Jan. You know we've had some problems and we're working on them. One way we've decided to do that is to give the whole family a new beginning. And this is the life we want for you and Josh. For ourselves."

"I liked it the way it was," Jan said in a small voice. "My old school. My old friends."

"You've made that abundantly clear." Karen raised one eyebrow. "But you aren't the only person in the world, Jan. And you don't necessarily know now how you'll feel six months from now, or six years." Karen finished her coffee and put her mug in the sink. They'd been sitting in the kitchen at the round white table in front of the French doors that led to the deck. Karen brushed imaginary crumbs off the front of her white linen pants, a habitual gesture whenever she stood up from the table. Jan's mom always ate in delicate little bites, leaning over the plate if she were eating something drippy or crumbly. Jan was the one who dribbled spaghetti sauce or Miracle Whip on herself.

Karen fished her car keys out of her purse and jingled them. "I'm going to see Mom. Want to come? Josh will be at Kevin's all afternoon."

Jan looked down at her hands on the table edge and shifted uncomfortably in her chair. "I guess not. Not today. I might call Jess or Amy. Maybe meet at the mall. Try to make friends and all. Like you said." Jan hated herself. Coward.

But the halls at Gram's nursing home smelled like floor cleaner. Gram's mouth was lopsided, and spit dribbled out. And Jan's mom acted so cheerful. Like everything was fine. Jan bounced the Coke can impatiently, feeling the liquid slosh inside. If she loved

Gram, she ought to go see her. Jan half stood up, then sank back down. She listened to the garage door opening and closing and the sound of her mom's car fading into the distance.

Grown-ups could be so fake, Jan thought, so disgusted that her last swallow of Coke went partway up her nose and left her spluttering. It was hard to say who she was really mad at—her mom or herself. Jan told herself it was her mom. At the way she refused to see Jan's problem. The way she just smoothed everything over and made Forest Grove sound like paradise. Her parents had no clue how painful it was to belong nowhere at all.

Married people had their difficulties, sure. Jan remembered the huge fight her mom and dad had had six months ago at the old house. For a week her dad had stayed at a hotel while they "made some decisions." But then her parents started going for counseling and things settled down.

Jan had tried to learn what had happened. "What's wrong, Mom? Did Dad do something?"

"I just don't want to get into it, Jannie. But neither of us wants you and Josh to worry. We both love you and you know that."

Jan had nodded. Her friend Lucy had told her
about marriage counselors. She said that's what counselors told you to say—reassure the kiddies. What
Jan had wanted was to know what the problem was.
Shapeless fears were the worst. Back then, at least,
she'd had friends to talk to.

Lucy's parents were divorced. "They just didn't get
along anymore. It was like they got bored, I guess."
Lucy made a face. "At first it's awful. Then you get
used to it. I kept thinking they'd get back together,
hoping like at Thanksgiving and all. But then Dad got
married to Stephanie and they had Jon and it was just
two families and I hardly ever thought about it's ever
being different."

"It would be nice having two families," Jan had
said, trying to be supportive. The thought of shuffling
between two places that way made her feel cold all
over. In a few weeks, though, her mom and dad had
gotten into discussing kitchen cabinets and colors for
bathrooms and stuff for the new house they were buying. Would people planning to break up buy an expen-
sive new house? It wouldn't make sense.

Jan finished her drink and squeezed the can, feeling
a certain satisfaction at the soft metal crumbling in

her fingers. She unclenched her hand and looked at the wrinkled red-and-white aluminum, the letters crunched together. It was a bright sunny Saturday in July. And what was she doing? Hanging out in her kitchen listening to the air conditioning hum. Her frustration made Jan feel prickly, as if she'd fallen into a patch of thistles. The sun coming in through the mini-blinds made stripes on her arm. The refrigerator motor started up.

Jan looked over the wet bar that separated the kitchen from the great room and felt a little dizzy at the space, stretching past the fireplace to the big bay windows at the front, soaring two stories up to the rough-hewn beams, which her mom and dad had explained were actually Styrofoam. The old house had had a family room in the basement, with shag carpeting. It was snug down there. "You don't find family rooms as such in the newer homes," Karen had told Jan. "Great rooms are more multipurpose, and they are so much more impressive. Isn't this room gorgeous?" Jan had had to grant that it was. And the formal living room off the foyer to the left was, too. The whole house would have impressed almost anybody. Jan stretched and stood up, crossed the room in front of the fireplace, and sank onto the sofa. Dust motes danced in the light streaking in from the round window high above the front entranceway. Jan watched them, bright specks just floating aimlessly this way and that.

Problems

It was the day of the first tennis tournament. The stands at
the club were packed with parents and kids from the
neighborhood. Jan's dad and mom were there, smiling
and waving. Jan was determined to do everything
right. She stretched way up to serve, on her tiptoes,
tossed the ball up, and swung. There were no strings
in her racket. It was like a basketball hoop. The ball
went whizzing through it. Jan tossed a second ball and
swung again. The same thing happened. And, getting
desperate, she tried again. Still no strings. Amy was
on the other side of the net, waiting. The more Jan
tried, the more Amy just grinned, taunting her. Finally
it got dark and everybody left. Still Jan was there, mesmerized, batting the ball with a circle of empty air.

She was all alone. The net on the court was hopelessly far away. She saw it, a dim white line in the distance. The court had grown bigger than a football field, dark and shapeless as a desert, and she was at one end swinging her arm up, flailing the darkness with her useless racket.

Jan woke up, sweating. She told herself it was just a dream. Dreams never made sense.

She sat on the side of the bed, rubbing the bottoms of her feet on the plush carpet. She needed to go to the bathroom for a glass of water. The hum of voices drifted up from below. Mom and Dad back from the club. Jan stood for a minute, groggy, comforted by the sound. At night, Jan always felt good when they came home and she knew she wasn't the one in charge anymore. The shadows in the yard were still unfamiliar, hunching dark shapes like men in ski masks.

Jan padded into the bathroom and ran the water until it was cold. She didn't bother to turn on the lights, just stood in the dark and listened to the water run. This bathroom, with its fluffy rug by the shower and its elegant row of makeup lights over the vanity, this whole bathroom was hers. It was so private. Nobody would stumble over her lash-extender gel and make fun of her. Josh wouldn't come pounding on the door the minute she started to blow-dry her hair. She could push up her breasts in front of the mirror, seeing if they were big enough yet for her to have real cleavage, comfortable that no one would yell at her through the door.

After she gulped down the water, Jan started to go back to bed. The voices from downstairs were louder, their rhythm speeded up. Mom and Dad were fighting. Jan shut her eyes and swallowed hard. Oh why couldn't they just shut up and go to bed? In the morning maybe they'd forget about the argument. Jan opened her door a crack.

"You can't—"

"How will—"

"Tell me what—"

Little broken bits were all that floated up to her. Jan strained to sort out the words. Mesmerized, she drew closer to the sounds, walking softly down the hall to the stairs. Halfway down, where the landing turned, she crouched against the wall.

"Look, Ken, forget it. How could you possibly think I could put up with something like that?"

"They were all the way on the other side of the room, Karen. Anyway, how was I supposed to know?"

"That's hard for me to believe. Really hard. That you wouldn't have thought that she'd be there."

"I'm not her social secretary. I don't know who all Allyson's friends are, for Christ's sake."

"You slept with her. It's reasonable to assume you know her."

"Karen, I've told you it's over. How long will it take you to believe that? You know I'm telling the truth. The thing is, you don't *want* to believe me. You're *enjoying* it in some weird way. I swear I'm starting to feel that. Otherwise, you'd give me a chance. Are you getting some kick out of playing the martyr? Is that it?"

"Where do you get off feeding me all that psychobabble, you self-righteous bastard?" Karen was sobbing, long rasping sobs that Jan thought would have torn her lungs loose.

"I didn't know she was coming tonight. The last thing I wanted was to run into her. And I'm sure she didn't know we'd be there, either."

"Ken, listen to what you're saying. Allyson couldn't have *planned* to ruin our evening. You're defending her. The blond floozy. I'm the hysterical victim. You and Allyson have the parts of the rational adults."

"Karen, I avoid her at work. She's two floors down. I never see her. What harm can she do?"

"She can follow me around like a disease. You remember that video? *Fatal Attraction?* I feel like Michael Douglas's wife."

"Forget the movies, Karen. Let's deal with the real world, at least. Allyson was as embarrassed as we were. I know she'd never have come if she knew—"

"Oh really? I thought you just said you weren't her social secretary, that you hardly knew her. Now you're sure just what she's feeling."

"Karen, you're impossible. I made a mistake, a serious mistake. I said I was sorry. What do you want? How long do I go on groveling?"

Jan couldn't listen anymore. She felt out of breath, like somebody had hit her in the stomach, and her ears were ringing. Gripping the rail, she lurched up the stairs and crept into her room, pushing the door until the latch clicked and the sound of voices was muffled to an indistinct blur.

She didn't know what to do. Get back into bed or sit in her window seat or go to the bathroom? She sat on the floor next to the wall, hands wrapped around her knees, and tried to think. How could her dad have been with somebody else? She pictured him the way she saw him every morning, leaning over to kiss her mom on the cheek, on his way out the door. The two of them, dressed up for dinner at the club, that special shine on them that she'd always thought was happiness. The way they'd talked about kitchen cabinets and kinds of window frames and all that, finishing the new house.

Never, ever in her worst nightmares had Jan ever thought her dad might have been with another woman. Jan had thought she wanted to know what was wrong. She'd asked her mom to tell her. But this wasn't the kind of problem that she knew the answer to. This was like the tennis court that lost its lines and edges and grew bigger and bigger until she was left alone flailing the dark with her stringless racket.

Jan didn't want to think about her parents' sex lives. When Jan first learned how it happened, she thought it had to be wrong. At least about her mom and dad. Even as old as she was now, she found she still had some of that dumb disbelief. They ought to be past all that.

And now, her dad with somebody else? Somebody named Allyson? From his office? *With* this other woman? She saw him in a restaurant, leaning across the table toward a blond woman—looking intent the way he did when he was asking her mom what she wanted on the menu. Jan shut her eyes and tried to be reasonable. Divorces weren't the end of the world. She'd still see her dad on weekends, holidays. That's the way it worked for Lucy and lots and lots of kids. She and Josh would learn to deal with it.

Somehow, those thoughts weren't a comfort. Lucy's experience didn't help. What kind of world was it when your own parents betrayed each other? How could Jan account for that and still have any rules, any kind of edges or boundaries in her world? "Don't panic," she whispered to herself out loud, and then again, since the sound of a voice, even her own, was a comfort just then. "Don't panic."

Jan should never have made such a big deal about going to Monica's. Not with what her mom was going through. Jan should never have griped when they first suggested she baby-sit Josh all summer.

Jan hated her dad. She couldn't stop seeing the ugly picture of him at a restaurant table, smiling at a strange woman. Jan went back to the bathroom and threw up. She rinsed her mouth and spat out the water. She was shaking.

Jan walked back across her carpet to the bed. The room was familiar and not familiar. It wasn't comforting the way her old one had been. The old room had a smell she was used to, a musty, faintly rose-petal smell that had seeped into its pores. In the old room, traffic noise had lulled Jan to sleep. This room smelled like new carpet and was silent as a tomb. Jan hugged her knees and pulled the sheet around her. The quiet roared in her ears like a seashell, punctuated by a faint rhythmic swish from the ceiling fan.

Gram. That's who she wanted. Foolishly, she had a terrible longing to curl up on Gram's lap, the way she had when she was younger than Josh. Gram always made Jan feel safe. Jan used to test her, say mean things or naughty words to watch her reaction. "You don't mean that," Gram would say. "Not my Jan." She wanted to tell Gram what was happening, hear her explain. But, of course, nobody could upset Gram now, not after her stroke. And Gram had to struggle to talk anyway.

Jan tried to imagine what Gram might say if she

could talk to her. "Your mom and dad are good people. They love you and Josh. They'll work it out, you'll see." Jan could hear her saying that. But much as she tried to imagine Gram's gentle voice continuing to speak, she couldn't. The curtains stirred in the breeze from the ceiling fan; a dog barked outside; no words came.

Jan got up and went to use the bathroom. Then she came back and crawled into bed. She kept expecting to cry, but she didn't. Would her dad still be there in the morning? But, then, her mom had known about this for months. *Problems.* When her mom had told her they were having problems, could Jan have possibly been expected to think of something like this? Her mom worked so hard selling houses, organized the schedule for the family, kept in great shape, and dressed in perfect taste. How could her dad even think about another woman? And Jan herself had been a hog, arguing and arguing about looking after Josh. Jan swore she'd be a different person from that night on.

She heard water running somewhere in the house. Her mom and dad were going to bed. She wondered if her dad was in the guest room. At least they weren't still downstairs fighting. And no car had started up. She tried relaxing her muscles one at a time, the way the tennis coach had told the class to do if they got tensed up. Start with your toes and just gradually move up, one muscle at a time, let yourself sink into the mattress. When she got to her stomach, it was harder. It wouldn't quite unknot. But when her shoulders relaxed, she felt her whole upper body sag almost peacefully. Still, her mind whirled. She needed to make herself think about something else. This summer her mind often drifted to *Life Begins Again*, the soap opera she'd started watching, home all day minding Josh and his friend Kevin. Jan had never expected to find herself hooked on a soap, but once she saw it a time or two, she couldn't miss the show. The people in Port Henry were almost a second set of family and friends.

On the show, wives and husbands fell in love with other people and almost broke up all the time. In fact, the main couple on *Life Begins Again*, Dr. Tricia and Jeff Lord, were just making up after Jeff had been seeing somebody else. Like her mom and dad, Tricia and

Jeff were trying to work things out. But their life was further complicated because an unknown killer was stalking Tricia.

Jan had stood, last Friday, paralyzed, holding her yellow sock with glitter on it that she'd just pulled from under the bed. Jan often more or less cleaned up her room while she watched the show, so she could claim she just happened to have the set on, in case Josh burst in. She didn't want Josh and Kevin to know she always watched it. Josh might tell Mom. Her mom might tell her dad and he might pull her TV. He had these fits of ordering her and Josh to read library books every year or so. Usually after report cards came out. In a couple of weeks he'd forget about it, but Jan didn't want the hassle. And she didn't want to miss a minute of *LBA*.

"No," Jan had gasped out loud last Friday and then sunk onto the bed, helpless, as Dr. Tricia Lord had put the key in the ignition and begun the drive to the Lord mansion. Jan had seen anonymous, black-gloved hands tamper with the car. Jan knew Tricia was likely steering toward her own death.

Jan hugged her pillow and tried to imagine what

would happen Monday. Would there be an awful wreck? She could imagine the ambulance crew's astonishment on seeing Tricia, slumped behind the wheel, white as a sheet and unconscious. They'd lift her, limp as a doll, onto a stretcher. The siren would scream as the ambulance sped toward Central Hospital and the ER. Jan closed her eyes, imagining the horror of the ER staff when they recognized the still form on the stretcher. "Oh no . . . it can't be . . . it's Tricia Lord, *Dr.* Tricia Lord." Just as Nurse Lorrie Babcock picked up the phone to call Jeff with the terrible news, Jan drifted off to sleep.

The Mall

The next morning Jan came down while her mom was in the kitchen making coffee. Josh was eating cereal in the great room. Her dad wasn't up yet.

"Want to go to the mall, Mom? Or to the plant place to pick up some new bushes?" Three weeks ago, her mom had asked her to go to the nursery to shop for shrubs for the front yard. Jan had been bored stiff by the thought of bushes.

Her mom paused, a tablespoon of coffee poised over the filter. "No, Jan. Thanks. But I took care of that. And Dad's been doing the landscaping."

"Well, we could do something else," Jan said awkwardly. "Bike out on the trail. It's a nice day."

Her mom frowned, looking puzzled. "Gee, sweetie,

what a nice idea. But you know how it is . . . I've got showings scheduled all afternoon. Everybody wants to buy a house in the summer; it's my busy time."

"Sure, Mom. I know." Jan was kicking herself. Now her mom was probably feeling guilty about not spending time with her. Jan fixed a bowl of cereal and ate slowly. There was a hard lump in her stomach. She poured on more milk but that didn't help. Then she realized she had to hurry, so she wouldn't run into her dad. He always slept late Sundays, then spent hours reading the paper. With any luck he'd go out and play golf. As soon as she ate, she rinsed her bowl and stuck it in the dishwasher. Then she dashed back to her room and shut the door, but opened it a few inches when she heard voices downstairs.

"Where's Jan?" she heard her dad ask Josh. "She looking after you?"

"Jan's a grouch. She won't let anybody near her room, even if it's important." Josh sounded breathless, the way he always did when he was indignant. "I wanted her to help find my robot car that we packed in one of those boxes in the basement. You know what she said? 'Get lost.' She's mean. I hate her." Josh knew Jan was his big sister. That meant she was supposed to help him if he asked nicely. Jan remembered that feeling—that you knew just how everything was supposed to be.

"Later, Josh, OK? I'm getting some coffee now. Go play with your Nintendo." Jan heard her dad opening the kitchen cabinet, looking for a mug. Then, almost immediately, his voice again. "You want to catch some golf on TV later, Josh? We can do some practice-putting later."

"Nah, I think I'll go to Kevin's. His mom is letting us use his pool this afternoon."

"OK, if you've got something to keep you busy." Jan heard the hurt in her dad's voice. For a second she felt sorry for him. But only for a second. If he wanted to be friends with Josh, really, he'd do something Josh liked. Not all the time be after him to watch golf or football or learn to putt. When her dad tried to talk to Jan, he was often a little clumsy, making jokes or asking about sports and schoolwork, as if he had to look for a "topic."

"How's school?" he'd say. "Learn anything interesting today?"

What was a sane person supposed to say to that? Jan felt foolish, thinking how she'd made allowances

for her dad, been proud that he had so many important things on his mind that he forgot little details
about her and Josh sometimes. She'd pictured him
standing at the front of a conference room, telling the
other insurance executives his plans for making more
and more money. Well, she thought, guess what he
was really thinking about? Allyson. The name made
Jan picture frizzy curls, one of those women who laugh
all the time at nothing. Jan walked to the hall railing.
To yell down, "How's Allyson, Dad? Your girlfriend.
You called her yet this morning?"

She stood there, trembling, her cold hand on the
wooden banister. He'd kill her. She turned and went
back to her room, bursting into tears at the click of
the door closing. She threw herself across the bed
and sobbed.

After a few minutes, Jan wiped her face and blew
her nose. She thought of calling Lucy or Monica, but
she didn't have the number at the lake for Monica,
and Lucy she'd already talked to this week. Her mom
said she could make only one long-distance call a
week. So what could she do?

Jan thought of Jess and her kind smile. She was
almost a friend. Jan had to be with somebody.

"Hi," she said when Jess got on the phone. "This is Jan. You want to come over? Hang out over here for a while?"

"Gee, I'd like to. But I told Amy I'd go to the mall this afternoon. Meet us, why don't you? We're just going to get a drink, sit around. Window-shop."

"I've got some baby-sitting money. I wanted to get a new outfit."

"Great! We'll help you pick it out." Jess sounded genuinely glad she'd called. Jan was almost smiling when she hung up.

"I'm meeting some friends at the mall, Dad," she said on her way out, not looking into the great room, where she knew he was buried behind the newspaper. "I'll be back when Mom is, around four or five." She hoped he caught that—she was out of the house if he was in it. Back for her mom. But he rattled the paper and called, "OK. I may head out myself for a couple of hours. Have fun, Jannie." The door clicked behind her as he started to say something else. Jan left him in there talking to himself and got her bike out of the garage.

*   *   *

As soon as she stepped through the big glass doors into the mall's entrance court, Jan felt lighter. The big space soared above her; light flooded in, but the sun was no longer hot. Seasons were all the same in here, and time faded. It always seemed to be about two o'clock in the afternoon in malls, no matter when you went. Two o'clock on a kind of enchanted day when everything was bright and new and beautiful. Two o'clock was when her soap came on.

To meet Jess and Amy by the fountain, Jan needed to go through Dayton's furniture department. An emerald leather sofa was casually draped with a bright-colored throw—dark green with bright yellow-and-rose birds—as if someone had just put down her book and run to answer the phone. Suppose her mom and dad got a sofa like that for in front of the fireplace? And the two chairs in burgundy that were so huge you could curl up in them. And then put that big glass table with the squatty wooden legs in the middle? For bowls of popcorn when the family all gathered around the fire in the winter? Jan saw the four of them, laughing at her dad's jokes, teasing her mom. Her dad would ruffle up Josh's hair. Her mom and dad would reminisce about how they met and first went out and all. They'd play old seventies music. Her mom and dad would dance. Jan would pull Josh up and start teaching him to dance and they'd all laugh. As she looked at the Dayton's furniture, the scene came into focus, clear and bright as a TV sitcom.

Coming out into the concourse, Jan was smiling. She hurried past Ralph Lauren and Cratecraft World, the coffee store, and Waldenbooks, where there was a cool display of Nintendo games she'd have to tell Josh about. Jess and Amy were waiting, sitting beside the fountain on the bench outside Benetton.

"Jeez," Amy said. "At last. We were about to dial nine-one-one."

"I'm sorry. Isn't it the time you said?" Jan looked at her watch, then caught herself. Amy always made people feel like dorks.

"We came early," Jess said. "Shut up, Amy." Jess smiled at Jan. "Wanna guess who's here?"

Jan felt her stomach flutter. From that gleam in Jess's eye, she thought she knew: Steve Hauser, one of the caddies at the club. He was fourteen and tall and quiet, and they'd talked to him after tennis two or three times. Jan had caught him looking at her, then blushing and looking away. She'd juggled her racket from one hand to the other, light as a feather, with a little smile on her lips, easy and sure as Amy.

"I can't imagine. Who?" Jan heard the brittle edge to her voice and swallowed. She faked a yawn. "Whuuh. I barely slept last night. So what's the big deal?"

"We ran into Steve Hauser and some other guys. Over by the software place. I said we were meeting you. I bet we run into them."

"He's cute," Jan said. "But I don't know if I like him. I barely know him." She wiped her suddenly sweaty hands on her jeans.

"You like him." Amy laughed. "Hands a little sweaty?" She never missed anything. "Relax, he likes you, too."

"It's hot outside," Jan snapped. "That's why I'm sweaty. Do you really think so, though? Do you really think he likes me?"

"Give me a break. You know he does." Amy was going with a guy named Keith. Once he came over to watch them practice. He was really good-looking, but Jan didn't find out what he was really like. He just talked to Amy.

"Steve's nice," Jess said. "He used to cut our grass."

The girls wandered along, looking in the shops. "I've just got thirty bucks," Jan said. Three tens in her wallet had seemed like plenty of money at home. Looking at the price tags, though, made her think maybe she should have waited another week or two to shop.

The Gap had a sale rack of knit dresses. They went in and flipped through them. Jan found a blue trapeze-cut dress, just above knee length, that said to her, "Forest Grove." It would go with layers, tights, and clunky sandals. Or she could wear it plain. Amy had a dress sort of like it, but with sleeves. Jan held it against herself and looked in the mirror.

"Try it," Jess said. With all three of them crammed into the dressing room, it was hard for Jan to back far enough away to get the perfect view. What she liked as much as anything, though, was the way the dress felt. Slinky against her body, swaying if she turned. They spilled out into the store and Jan checked in the three-way mirror. The color made her eyes greenish blue and she was sure she saw coppery undertones in her hair she'd never noticed before. She swirled a couple of times, pretending she was checking the hem in the back, but really wanting to feel the dress flow around her body. Jan was only five feet four and not fat, but she worried she wasn't thin, either. In the dress, she felt as tall and slim as Amy.

"You can wear it lots of places," Jess said. "It's casual, but it'd be good for the first dance in the fall, while it's still hot."

Jan looked around at Amy for a last opinion, but she was trying on belts in front of the other mirror—the kind with shiny dangles that hang around your hips. Anyway, Jan knew it was the dress she needed. She tilted her chin and looked back at herself, a quick glance over her shoulder, trying to catch herself from an unexpected angle. There was a drama, a kind of mystery about her in the blue knit dress.

Jan saw herself floating down the staircase, her hand just touching the banister, with Steve standing at the bottom, looking up at her. Girls on dates always did that on TV commercials. Her dad would be there, reading the paper. A dog was usually in the picture, too. A nice family dog that wagged its tail and made everybody smile. Her first real date. "Is that you?" Josh would blurt out and her parents would look at each other, misty-eyed but laughing.

After she paid for the dress, Jan felt different just because she was carrying it in its plastic bag. She walked lightly, on the balls of her feet, and a sultry little smile hovered on her lips. The girls wandered toward the food court, where they found Steve and three of his buddies. They all sat at a round table with a striped umbrella and drank pop.

"You like caddying?" Jan leaned over her straw, letting her brown hair, cut in a smooth flip, slide onto her cheeks. Then she tossed her head and smiled.

"I like the money," Steve said, smiling back. "And it's outside. Last year I helped my mom at her shop. I hated being cooped up that way."

"I baby-sit my little brother. And his friend."

"Keep you hopping, huh? You order the little tikes around?"

"I'm mean," Jan said, grinning and lowering her eyelashes. She hoped the gel was working.

"Your folks just moved here?"

"Yeah. We lived in the city before. But it's nice out here."

"Kind of dull sometimes. I mean, there's the movies and the mall and that's about it. The city has to have a lot more." Steve shook the hair out of his eyes. He had a long-on-one-side haircut that slid over his eyebrow. He ran his hand through it.

"It's six of one and half a dozen of the other." Jan waggled her straw between her fingers. "I mean, there's advantages to the city, sure. But it's so pretty out here. It's hard, though, making new friends."

"Naah. For you? You'll see. Kids out here are real friendly." Steve reached out and squeezed Jan's shoulder. She smiled at him. Moving her foot forward, she bumped the plastic bag with her new dress. The afternoon was turning out perfect.

"Doesn't your dad play golf? Mr. McIver? Tall guy with dark hair?"

"Yeah." Jan felt her smile fade. "He's big on that."

"He's nice," Steve said. "I met him last week. He's over a lot."

"He practically lives there. I don't get it—whacking

that little ball around all day. I mean, how much fun can it be?" Jan preferred to talk about golf instead of about her dad. And how swell he was.

"What're you doing, then? With a tennis racket?"

"Well, but you've got people hitting it *back*. Golf just looks so boring. Half of it is waiting around for your turn."

"It's a businessman's game," Steve said. "Myself, I like speed. You ski?"

"I'm going to learn soon. We might go for a weekend this winter. My mom was saying maybe over Thanksgiving." Nobody had mentioned a ski trip, but Jan figured she might suggest it herself. A ski lodge might be romantic. Might even be a way to get her parents back together. In front of the fire and all. "I think it'd be a lot of fun. When do you go?"

"A couple of times a season. With my dad, usually, and my stepmother. We go out to Colorado."

"Gee." Jan wrapped her straw around her finger. "That's a long ways."

"It's great skiing. This year I'm trying snow-boarding."

"My cousin Larry has a jet ski." What did that have

to do with anything? Jan felt dumb. But she'd felt kind of out of her depth, talking about flying to Colorado. She and Monica and Lucy used to slide down the hill in the park on the plastic lids of their garbage cans. It was fun, wobbling and spilling out into the snow, trying to steer by shifting their weight. But snowboards? Jan wasn't even totally sure what they were.

"Does he?" Steve looked a little puzzled. "That's nice."

"I never rode it," Jan said, feeling herself getting in deeper. "I just heard he had one."

After a pause, Steve said politely, "You got a big family?"

Jan shook her head. "Just my mom and dad and brother. And my gram. Everybody else is out west or someplace."

Kids were starting to stand up. They all had finished their drinks. "It was nice talking to you," Jan said. Then blushed. She shouldn't have said that, should she? It had started out so great, talking to Steve. Then she'd brought up her cousin Larry for no reason and started sounding like a dork.

"I liked talking to you," Steve said. "I'll call you

later. You in the book? On the members' list at the club?"

Jan nodded.

"Great. Talk to you later."

Jan stooped down and picked up the magic bag with her Forest Grove dress. The three girls waved to the guys and headed for the doors to the outside. Jan swung her bag from one finger by its loop and floated down the concourse, under the big skylights, past the potted trees and the big entrance fountain spraying rainbows. The girls clanked open the bars on the doors to the parking lots. The heat rushed against Jan's body, a sudden oppressive weight. For a minute Jan was bewildered. What was this noisy world with car doors slamming and no background music, simmering in the sun? Sweat started to bead on her upper lip. A candy wrapper blew across the sidewalk at her feet. "See ya," she called to Jess and Amy. Jan pedaled home quickly. After time spent in the mall, the world outside seemed blurred, like an out-of-focus movie.

The Intimate Dinner

Sunday night Steve didn't call. Jan hadn't really expected he would that early, but still she ran to get the phone whenever it rang. In case. Her dad fixed hamburgers on the grill, and they brought them inside so they could watch *60 Minutes*.

"You have a nice day, Jannie?" her mom asked during a commercial.

"I hung out with Jess and Amy. We shopped at the mall."

Her mom smiled. "That's great, sweetie. Forest Grove's not the end of the world after all, huh?"

"I like it, Mom. The kids are really nice."

"Just watch you don't turn into a mall rat." Her

dad grinned at her. Jan looked away. There was an uncomfortable silence. He ought to be getting the message, Jan figured. Start leaving her alone with his stupid jokes.

"I want a pool," Josh said. "Kevin's mom says swimming's good for you."

"Someday, Josh," Jan's mom said.

"When? Kevin's has a diving board. I jumped off it."

"Hush, son." Jan's dad picked up the remote and turned up the sound. There was a story on *60 Minutes* about health insurance. Her dad wanted the government out of the insurance business. He took a hamburger from the platter and doused it with ketchup. He took a bite, staring at the screen. A plump red-haired girl needed a new heart but nobody wanted to pay for it. "That's the price you pay," her dad said, "for the best health-care system in the world. Believe me, if the government starts tinkering, none of us will be getting heart transplants."

"Still," Karen said stiffly, "I feel sorry for that little girl and her family."

Jan peeled back the top of her hamburger bun to squeeze on some mustard. Jan knew her mom agreed with her dad about big government and all that. For sure, her mom was needling him. Jan licked her finger and made a big point of turning away from the TV, looking bored.

Monday morning Steve didn't call either. Jan hadn't thought he would; you don't expect people to call in the morning, really. Even if she did happen to know that he worked afternoons and evenings. And it was still pretty early to hear from him. But all morning, while Jan loaded the breakfast dishes in the dishwasher and sorted the laundry and helped Josh and Kevin look for the robot car in the basement, all that morning, Jan did listen for the phone. Once she dashed to get it, but it was just a client, looking for her mom. Steve had said he would call and Jan thought he would, for sure. But at the back of her mind were some tiny doubts. Remembering Cousin Larry and his stupid jet ski, she felt her face get hot. Did that make Steve think she was weird? Still, it was after she'd said that that he'd said he'd call.

By two o'clock, when *Life Begins Again* was finally on, Jan was dying to stretch out and hang on every moment of it. All her worries vanished while she watched.

For an hour Jan was there with the characters, in another world.

Tricia Lord was OK. By a miracle, her car had been caught in a thick tangle of vines and had not plummeted off the cliff. All the viewer had seen so far was a pair of black-gloved hands, but that in itself led Jan to feel it was a professional job. Emma Martin, the private investigator, had confirmed that view. "Definitely the work of a professional," she'd said, shaking her lovely waist-length chestnut hair, "and a very clever professional at that."

Her partner, Mike Burton, concurred. "It's possible we're dealing with a trained assassin. A cold-blooded killer." Jan shivered when she heard Mike say that, but there was no other explanation. The way the guy knew how to fix wires and all. The question was, why would *anybody* want to kill Tricia? All the student nurses loved her; she and Lorrie Babcock were the most popular people on staff at Central—both so down-to-earth and friendly and nice to everybody.

These attacks were coming at the worst possible

time, when Jeff and Tricia were trying to put their marriage back together after he had been seeing Charlotte Winthrop in a brief affair, which meant nothing compared to his feelings for Tricia. Tricia and Jeff had both had affairs from time to time, but really they loved each other. Anybody could see how they felt about each other. Now, in addition, they were expecting their son, JL, back from school in Switzerland so that the three of them could be a family again. Monday's program started on the Lord yacht—a romantic dinner Jeff had planned just for Tricia and himself. An intimate dinner for them to rediscover their feelings for each other.

"You know you mean everything to me, Tricia. You and JL." Jeff pulled Tricia closer to him on the leather sofa. A gleaming silver bucket held a bottle of champagne. In the background was a table set with white linen and covered silver dishes containing the intimate dinner for two. "Charlotte was never anything to me, Tricia. Not the way you are."

"I know, Jeff. Since Charlotte went back to Zack, I've had time to think about what means the most to me. You do, Jeff. I know that now. Everything would be perfect if—"

He put his finger to her lips. "Everything *is* perfect, my love. You have the best protecting you—they don't come any better than Emma and Mike. Let them do the worrying. You have to get on with your life."

"You know I've forgiven you, Jeff. You know, if something happens . . . that I've always loved you. Since all this began I haven't been a wife to you in the way—"

Again, he stopped her speaking, this time with a kiss. "I can't forgive myself for the pain I've caused you. All that is about to change, my love. Tonight is a new beginning. We can't let this brutal assassin make any difference in our relationship." He went over to the entertainment center and pushed a button. As music flooded the state room, Jeff pulled Tricia to her feet and drew her close. They danced, tight in each other's arms. After a few minutes, Jeff stooped and gathered Tricia up, her shapely legs kicking in high-heeled shoes like the ones Jan's mom wore when she was dressed up.

"Jeff! What about the dinner?"

"We'll have that for dessert, my sweet." Jeff swept her out the swinging door at the end of the long room, a door inscribed, as all the doors on the yacht were, with the gold crest of the Lord dynasty. On the way, he stooped and pulled a single red rose from a crystal bud vase, passing it to the laughing Tricia, who held it to her nose.

Jan was melting. With difficulty she pulled herself back to the present and her job minding Josh and Kevin. While a Charmin toilet tissue commercial was on, she went to the door and listened. She heard the *swishes* and *zooms* and *pows* that accompanied firing various weapons in the Magic Sorcerer game. Josh wouldn't be bothering her during the show. She sank back against the pillows.

The next scene showed Emma and Mike working late at the office, desperately using their computers to access Global Security Network data to see if they could uncover any evidence to help them identify the sinister black-gloved figure. Both of them were former secret agents with the GSN.

"We need more help with this, Mike," Emma said. "I'm afraid this job is too big for the two of us."

"Who can we trust on this one?" Mike shrugged his rugged shoulders. "In a case like this, *everyone* has to be a suspect. There've been two attempts; that last one—"

"Was obviously an inside job," Emma finished his thought. "Somebody knew her route. Somebody timed those brakes to fail just at the right moment— that can't have been an accident."

"We have to bring in somebody from the outside," Mike said. "Somebody who'll see things fresh, whatever we're missing."

"I'll do it!" Jan bounced up to a sitting position. Emma Martin turned and looked straight at her. Their eyes met. The screen dissolved. Jan was *there*. In Port Henry. After that Jan watched the commercials in a fog, getting her concentration back only for the last scene. Jeff and Tricia returned to the Lord mansion after their special evening on the yacht. Tricia paused beside the foyer table, startled to discover a bouquet of flowers.

"Jeff! It's the perfect touch. You thought of everything."

He shook his head. "I wish, my darling. But they

are not from me. Read the card. Let's see who your other admirer is."

As Tricia opened the little envelope, the joy drained from her face. Silently, she held the card out to Jeff.

"Enjoy life. While you can." Jeff's features contorted with rage as he read the cryptic message. The camera zoomed close on the bouquet—pink rosebuds around the edge, bluebells, and, in the center, spotted lilies, frothy as sea foam.

"How strange those lilies are." Tricia shuddered. "Covered with spots."

"This is a coward's attempt to frighten you. That's all."

"I'm tired of fear, Jeff," Tricia said bravely. "Tonight has been a new beginning. I'm not going to let anything spoil that." Tricia went into the living room and poured herself a snifter of brandy.

Alone in the hall, Jeff immediately went to the telephone, careful that Tricia wouldn't hear. "Emma? Can you get over here? There's been a new development." Quietly, he replaced the receiver and went in to Tricia. The music that ended the show began as he sank down beside his wife and smiled, concealing the anxiety that had shaken his voice moments before as he spoke to the private investigator who was attempting to prevent his wife's murder.

Jan clicked off the TV and reached for a tissue from the box beside the bed. Softly, comfortably, she sobbed. It was so moving seeing Jeff and Tricia back together, seeing Tricia so brave in the face of danger. Still, it wasn't that sad. She blew her nose and wiped her eyes. Really, she didn't know why she was crying.

Sunday Brunch

Jan clicked off the remote and leaned back against the pillows. What she needed was to think of something that would make her parents see how much they all meant to each other.

Jan didn't have a yacht, and an intimate dinner with silver covers was out. But how about a brunch? Jan pictured the four of them sitting on the great room floor by the big low table. With their plates heaped with pancakes, they were all laughing and talking at once, the aroma of freshly brewed coffee in the air. There was a commercial on TV every Christmas about a boy coming home while his family slept. He made coffee, and the smell wafted through the house, bringing everybody to the kitchen, hugging and kissing and smiling. Jan mulled over the idea, and it seemed better and better. A big Sunday breakfast in the great room might be just the eye-opener her parents needed.

"Oh, Ken, we have to put all that behind us."

"Karen, my love, you mean everything to me. You and the children." Jan closed her eyes and played the scene, her dad coming up behind her mom and enclosing her in a hug, her mom blushing and turning to snuggle against his chest.

The week was long and empty. Steve still hadn't called. And Jan was humiliated on Wednesday at tennis, knowing Amy was watching her from the next court but still not able to keep from glancing over at where the caddies waited outside the pro shop. She saw the back of somebody out on the course that might have been Steve, but she wasn't sure. Sometimes Jan was sure Steve was just being polite when he said he'd call. After she'd been such a freak and said "Enjoyed talking to you," or some dumb thing like that. But then she'd think that really he did seem to like her. Maybe he was out of town. Maybe he was sick.

Jan was playing Jess. Jess kept hitting shot after

shot right past Jan. Jan stood there stupidly while an easy shot landed at her feet and dribbled off the court. "It's not your day," Jess said, laughing. "Forget your contacts?" Jess was a good tennis player, but Jan wasn't so bad. The more Jan told herself she was going to pay attention to the game and forget about Steve, the worse she got. Once she even dropped her racket.

By then Jess's mom, Mrs. Werch, was in the stands, waiting to drive them home. "How are you, Jan?"she'd asked after the game, as though she felt sorry for Jan.

"Fine," Jan said stiffly. She needed to make some joke about being so klutzy, to blow it off, but she felt too miserable to think of one.

In that whole wretched, empty week, the only thing Jan enjoyed was planning the Sunday surprise brunch. It would be a wake-up call to her parents, a reminder of how much being a family meant to all of them. On Sunday Jan woke at eight and went downstairs. Her parents weren't up. Josh was in the great room watching cartoons and eating cereal.

"Don't drizzle that cereal around," she said automatically. "That pink stuff smears." Josh ate cereal without any milk, like a horse or something. She could hear the crinkling noise of his chewing from across the room. And he loved Sweet Puffs with the pink marshmallow stars that ground into the rug if somebody stepped on the ones he'd dropped. Their mom was always after him.

Looking at her brother, sitting cross-legged with his knees out and the bowl balanced against his almost nonexistent tummy, Jan felt a sudden pang that made her nose sting. Josh thought he was so safe in his small world. Jan wanted to protect him.

"Let's fix Mom and Dad breakfast, Josh," she said. "Surprise them."

"Huh?" Josh turned toward her, curious. "Fix them what?"

Normally people in Jan's family just got their own breakfast—her mom toasted a bagel; her dad ate Wheaties or frozen waffles he dropped in the toaster. Jan liked strawberry toaster tarts with white frosting.

She was uncertain how to begin. She measured out five heaping spoons of coffee, relishing the warm smell as she dipped the spoon into the can. She loaded up the coffee machine and flipped the switch. The aroma, as she'd intended, did waft into the great room, perhaps even drift to the second floor where her parents slept.

Josh came in to put his empty bowl in the sink. "How come you're doing that?"

"I just thought it would be nice. We could fix a brunch, like Mother's Day. To let them know we love them. That we're a family and all."

Josh laughed. "Girls are so dumb. What else could we be?" He stretched, seeing if he could touch the sink and the table at the same time, but his arms were still too short.

"You know what I mean," Jan said impatiently. "To say we *care*. I thought we could make pancakes."

Josh brightened. "Well, OK. I'll help. How do you do it? Show me."

Jan pulled the cookbook from the shelf over the sink. "I'll look it up."

Jan pushed the step stool over to help Josh reach the counter. She let him crack the egg into the bowl, then she fished out the pieces of shell with her finger. Josh got very serious once she let him help. He beat the egg with the wire whisk and they added milk and two tablespoons of oil. Jan measured the dry ingredients: a cup and a half of flour, a half teaspoon of sugar, and a teaspoon of salt. The recipe called for two teaspoons of baking powder. She looked all over. They didn't have any.

"What can we do, Josh? Without baking powder?" Her voice dipped toward a sob.

Josh looked at her and frowned. "What's wrong, Jannie?" She heard a tinge of fear in his voice.

Jan swallowed hard. She'd been picturing the scene when her parents came down—how pleased they'd be. She'd revised her plan, thinking they'd sit at the counter on the stools and she'd pass over heaping plates of golden cakes drenched in syrup, and steaming cups of coffee.

To have all that blotted out by two teaspoons of baking powder. It was too much. "I wonder if we could use baking soda?" she said. "There's some in the fridge. To keep it from smelling."

"Sure," Josh said. "Try it." He smiled at her reassuringly.

Jan sifted everything together and dumped it into the egg and milk while Josh stirred. "Keep stirring," she said. "Get rid of the lumps." Josh stirred a little too fast and splattered batter on the counter. Some ran down the cabinet doors, but not much. Jan had sifted some flour on the floor, but that would be easy to clean up.

She stooped and looked into the cabinet beside the dishwasher where the pots and pans were. "I need a griddle or a big frying pan," she said to Josh. "I know there's a big iron one that would work."

"What on earth?" Her mom's voice was so piercing that Jan bumped her head, turning to stand up.

She followed her mom's gaze. The kitchen did look kind of messy. The eggshell was still lying on the counter, and the other stuff was out: the milk carton, the oil. And there were the spills. "We're fixing you brunch," she said in a small voice. "You and Dad. For a surprise."

Her mom's face softened. "That's sweet, you two. And you made coffee. How wonderful." But her mom was speaking carefully, measuring every word. Jan's heart sank. Nothing had turned out. The scene was a mess instead of the happy breakfast she'd pictured. "It looks like it'll be delicious." Her mom took a swallow of the coffee. "And this coffee is perfect. Just what

I needed. But I can't stay for the rest. I'm sorry. I have two open houses. You know how it is on Sundays."

Sundays, especially in the summer, were very big for showing new houses. Jan knew that. She just hadn't thought. "Dad can eat it," Josh said. "Is he going to play golf today?"

"I don't know what your father's plans are," their mom said stiffly. "Tell him I'll be back by four." She patted Josh on the head and kissed Jan on the forehead. "What sweet kids," she said. "I'm lucky to have such sweet kids." Her eyes strayed to the counter.

"I'll clean up," Jan said. "You won't know there was ever any mess here at all." After her mom left, Jan took the batter and scraped it into the garbage disposal.

"Hey!" Josh grabbed her arm. "That's our pancakes. For Dad."

"They wouldn't turn out, Josh. Not without the baking powder." She turned on the water and flipped the disposal switch. The grinding noise was almost comforting, echoing through the still house. A faint trace of her mom's cologne was left in the air behind her—a delicate spicy smell. Jan used the sprayer to wash the last of the gummy batter down the drain.

Between Two Worlds

So the brunch was a disaster. And Steve still hadn't called. Monica was miles away at the lake, and Lucy went to camp. On Monday afternoon, Jan started to call Jess, but she put the phone back down. In the morning she'd herded Josh and Kevin to soccer, so she hadn't gotten to her chores. She went down to the basement and sorted the wash—three piles, dark, medium, and white—cold, warm, and hot. Her dad's socks smelled musty and Josh's soccer stuff was sweaty. Some of the underwear had gross yellow stains. Jan tried not to notice.

The house was full of smooth hummings and whirrings from the ceiling fans and the air conditioning and the dishwasher and the washing machine and dryer.

All day, Jan heard machines clicking efficiently. This morning it was the washer—changing to the spin cycle, briskly spraying water, sighing into silence. And upstairs in the great room, the *zooms* and *pows* of Josh's video games.

Jan went upstairs for more dirty laundry. Carrying the plastic baskets down the stairs, Jan found herself whispering under her breath. Talking to Emma and Mike. Warning Tricia about the unknown killer. Jan saw herself standing beside Dr. Tricia Lord in surgery, struggling to save Jess, who had been washed over a waterfall in a canoe on a vacation trip to a tropical island. If Jess lived, she might never walk again.

"Would she even want a life like that, Jan? She's always been so active." Jess's mom was distraught, depending on Jan, a young resident, to pull her daughter through.

"She has the best, Mrs. Werch. I've had Dr. Tricia Lord flown in, because I know if anybody can get Jess through this, she can."

"I'm so grateful, Jan. For everything." Mrs. Werch wiped her eyes and managed a brave smile.

Jan stuffed the next load of wash into the machine, pushed the button, and watched hot water spraying over the sheets. The hissing of the water broke the spell, and she was back in her own basement laundry room. The dimness of the room was unnerving. Jan rattled the washer lid, making as much noise as possible, and took the stairs up to the kitchen two at a time.

The central air conditioning hummed the slightest bit; it wasn't loud like the window units they'd had at the old house. "We'll have air, Jan," her mom had told her, describing the new house. Jan smiled. She'd thought everybody had air. The ceiling fan was going in the great room, where the boys were crouched in front of the big TV screen.

Jan went into the kitchen to unload the dishwasher. Her mom kept a schedule taped on the refrigerator so they could all figure out where everybody was. "It's insane, Pat," Jan had heard her mom telling a woman in her office recently. "We barely see each other, between Josh's soccer and Janet's tennis and Ken's and my late meetings. And his golf, and my mom . . . Is there an end to this, I wonder? When we can sit down together and be a family?"

Jan pushed the release bar and opened the dishwasher door. Listening to her mom say things like that, Jan got a picture of a happy, hectic life with all of them rushing to activities and yearning to spend time together. Being busy all the time, "on the go" her mom called it, that was what made a family count. Was her mom bragging when she talked that way? Was she lying? Jan couldn't fit the image that came from her mom's description with the one that filled her mind on days like today.

Still, it was all true. Jan's tennis, Josh's soccer—in the fall they'd both have piano again, too. Her mom's aerobics and visits to Gram and then both her parents had meetings. Besides their counseling sessions. So they *were* rushing places a lot. Why, then, did Jan keep flashing back to her dream?

Jan lifted the silverware rack onto the counter. The kitchen fork had sharp prongs. For no reason, she pressed the flesh of her thumb into the points. Pulling it off, she saw two tiny, bright drops of blood. Shaken, Jan hastily shoved the fork into the drawer.

"Quit feeling sorry for yourself." Jan unloaded the rest of the dishes quickly, determined to cheer herself up. She'd finished the chores for the day. Josh and Kevin were fine. She still didn't feel like calling anybody. She went up to her room, only to discover she couldn't even escape into *LBA*. They'd put a stupid news conference on instead. Without letting anybody know ahead of time. Jan lay on the bed, stunned, the remote useless in her hand. There had to be some way to redeem this Monday that was sliding from boring to disastrous. She thought about the dress she'd bought at the mall. Jan had just held it up in front of herself last week when she got home. She hadn't tried it on again.

Probably Steve and his family were on vacation. Or some relatives had come to visit. Or a thousand things might have kept him from calling. When he did call, Jan needed to be ready. If he asked her out, she needed to have tried on the dress and figured out if she should wear sandals or her new canvas boots.

Just as she had earlier, Jan pretended she was someone from TV. She was going to change before she dashed off to a fancy party or, even better, to a meeting in a chrome-and-glass office where everybody was waiting for her opinion. She was running late and every eye turned toward her when she took her place at the head of the polished table. She entered, wearing her blue dress, the smooth knit swirling around her body as she leaned over to pick up her charts.

Spreading the dress out on her chintz bedspread,

Jan frowned. The blue was darker than she remembered and, seeing it on the bed, she had to say it was kind of shapeless. But no dress looked great just lying on a bed. She put it on, smoothed her hair, and looked in the mirror on her bathroom door. Her legs were pale and lumpy like a plucked chicken's. And the color, without the glow of the mall lights, just sat there, blah, and turning her skin yellow.

Jan tried moving in sweepy model gestures, throwing out her hips, putting her hands up like she was reaching for something, pursing her lips, shaking her hair. Nothing helped. Was it the light? Jan sank to the bed. The dress had been so perfect at the mall. It didn't make sense. She peeled it off and hung it in her closet, toward the back so she wouldn't see it the minute she opened the door.

Had she bought it because Amy had one like it? Did she really look that awful? Jan collapsed across the bed and stared at the ceiling. Blinking back tears, Jan turned her thoughts to *Life Begins Again.* She'd almost been pulled into the screen last week when Emma and Mike talked about needing somebody from the outside to go undercover. She pictured herself in Emma's office. "Even the cleverest killer will slip up sometime," she heard herself saying to the two former secret agents. "I want to be there when this one does."

"You have the instincts of a pro, Jan," Mike told her after her first afternoon.

"She's taking to this like a duck to water!" Emma was already starting to think of Jan as somebody who could follow in her own footsteps. Somebody who thrived out on the edge.

After her first day undercover, Jan was going back to an apartment she shared with one of the student nurses—maybe Dawn, a really sweet girl with long blond hair. Back in the apartment, Jan barely had time to shower and change before Steve came by to take her to dinner. The buzzer sounded at the door and there he stood, tossing back his hair and smiling his slow smile. With an expression that said everything about how he felt about her, Steve handed her a single red rose.

"You've got to think about yourself, Jan," he said. "You're putting yourself in danger. This guy is playing for keeps."

Modestly, Jan brushed aside his worries. "It's nothing," she said. "I'm just back-up. Emma and Mike are the pros." They rode down in the elevator and climbed into Steve's cool car, a green 'Vette, on the way to the restaurant Mike's former partner had started. It was the most elegant place in Port Henry. They had a romantic table for two, set for an intimate dinner.

"We'll have champagne, please," Steve said to the waiter. "Your best." When it came, he proposed a toast. "To the bravest girl I know," he said, looking deep into her eyes. "And the most beautiful."

Jan blushed. "I don't deserve this, Steve," she said. "I'm just doing what anybody would do, trying to help."

The waiter brought covered silver dishes on a cart. Jan picked up the long-stemmed rose lying beside her plate and inhaled its fragrance, looking straight into Steve's eyes. He reached across the table and put his hand over hers.

"If anything happened to you, Jan," he said, a catch in his voice, "I don't think I could go on. Not without you."

"Nothing will happen," she told him bravely. "When I'm with you I feel so safe." She imagined how it would be later, in the car when he took her home, his arms around her, his lips on hers.

"Jan! Jan! Josh isn't playing fair!" Slowly Jan became conscious of screams and thuds from the great room.

"What is it?" She hurried downstairs as the yelling grew louder.

"It's my turn. You know it is!" Kevin was gripping Josh's T-shirt by the shoulders and pounding him against the back of the sofa.

"Cut it out. You're stretching that shirt all out of shape!" Jan pulled them apart. Both of them were panting. Their faces were red.

"So what?" Kevin was furious. "Who cares? He won't give me a turn."

"What's the problem?" Jan turned Josh loose, keeping her hand just over his shoulder in case she needed to grab him again. She kept her grip on Kevin.

"I want to be the Magic Sorcerer," Kevin said. "We're taking turns. He promised. He was, last time."

"Is that true, Josh?" He stuck out his lip slightly and got that defiant look he always did when he knew he was wrong. "It's my Nintendo. I understand how to be the Magic Sorcerer. Kevin is better being Prince Enrico."

"That's a joke," Kevin said. "Who blew it on level

three? Who got stuck in the labyrinth and completely forgot all about the spell to enchant the dragon?"

"Well, what about your magic sword? Who let the dragon escape in the first place? If you'd stuck him with your sword, the blade would have been poison."

"You stepped on that tree toad in the Enchanted Glade. That's why we got stuck in the labyrinth in the first place."

Jan almost laughed, but didn't want to hurt their feelings. They were so serious, you'd almost think they really were hanging out in glades and slaying dragons and casting spells. "Look," she said, "it's a *game*. You two aren't in a magic kingdom. You're right here, banging into the furniture. Cut it out. Right now. Josh"—she looked sternly at him, his skinny chest still heaving, his blue eyes blazing—"you aren't being nice. You know it's really Kevin's turn. You agreed."

"But I'm *better*—" Jan cut him short.

"Well, how's Kevin going to learn if you always hog the sorcerer part? Either Kevin is the sorcerer or you quit playing. I'll put that Nintendo game away and tell Mom you guys can't play it for a month."

Josh looked panicked. He knew she meant it. That

game was his life right now. Jan practically had to use dynamite to get the two of them to shut it off so they'd go to the park for soccer practice.

Kevin and Josh settled back down in front of the TV. Jan went into the kitchen to start lining up dinner. Her mom had left a menu beside the schedule on the refrigerator door—chop suey. Jan needed to thaw some hamburger in the microwave, then brown it, mix in a can of vegetables, and do some instant rice. There was a bag of toasted Chinese noodles. Her mom had already fixed a lime Jell-O dessert with layers of Kool Whip so it looked striped. Jan put four plastic mats on the table and set out the soy sauce. She got the stainless steel out of the drawer and put the forks and knives and spoons around. The phone rang. It was Kevin's mom. She was running late; Kevin would eat over. Jan set another place.

In half an hour her dad would be home. And then her mom. Looking at the table to see if she'd forgotten anything, Jan sighed. Why had her dad done such an awful thing? When he really did love her mom? He'd said he did, and Jan thought he was telling the truth. Couldn't it have been a momentary sort of thing?

Like he and Jan's mom had had a fight the way everybody does once in a while and then along comes
Allyson at just the wrong moment, when his guard
was down.

That happened a lot on *LBA*. Lorinda Easton
sashayed around in her skintight leotards with eency
leather skirts. Jan thumped the salt and pepper shak-
ers on the table. Lorinda begged a married man to
come over to help her fix a broken pipe or something
and what was she wearing when he got there? A black
teddy with see-through lace. Allyson must have strut-
ted her stuff past Jan's dad over and over and finally
he'd caved in.

"Hi, Jannie. How's my girl?" Dad came in through
the door from the garage and gave her a squeeze.
She'd been so lost in thought, she'd barely registered
the sound of his car and of the door going up. Jan's dad
was tall and his dark hair was thinning on top. He had
green eyes like hers and skin that freckled in the sun,
like Josh's. He always smelled like pine needles from
his deodorant and aftershave.

Sometimes Jan would see him staring off into the
distance with his glasses halfway down his nose, not
seeing anything. Ever since she was small, Jan had

wanted to ask him what he was thinking, but he'd always seemed too important, too far above her. Still, she'd understood that, like her, he was a dreamer. Josh and her mom were the practical ones. So Jan had felt a special connection to her dad. A connection that had dissolved once she found out that what he'd been dreaming about lately was probably Allyson. Despite herself, though, Jan found herself smiling at him, warming to his friendliness.

He peered in at Josh and Kevin. "Off in Never-Never Land, huh? Did you get them out today?"

"They had soccer this morning. At the park."

Her dad pulled off his tie and jacket and hung them on the back of a chair and went to the fridge for a beer. "Like a pop?"

"Sure. Thanks." They sat at the table with their drinks.

"How's the serve coming?"

"Better. It's my backhand that's the worse problem now."

"When's the first tournament? I'll mark it on my calendar."

"That's OK, Dad. You don't need to do that." Jan looked down at her pop can. "I know you're busy."

"Hey," he said, "I wouldn't miss it. A chance to see the new Steffi Graf." He grinned at her.

"I'm not that great."

"Well, you get out there and try and I'll come root for you."

Jan looked up and smiled at him. "You may be embarrassed," she said. "I'm warning you."

"I'll get a fake mustache," he said, "and a pair of dark glasses." They both laughed.

Her mom's car pulled up outside. They heard the door thud shut. Jan looked at her dad. His face tensed up, a tight little frown appearing between his eyes.

"Hi, everybody. What a hectic day!" Jan's mom came in with a paper bag of groceries. Her dad stood up to take them from her and put them on the counter. "Thanks, Ken. Everything under control, Jannie?"

"It's fine, Mom. Kevin's eating over. Dinner's almost ready. I waited to do the rice."

"Maybe we ought to let the boys eat in the other room with the Nintendo, Karen. You look done in."

"No, no." Her mom poured herself a glass of white wine and took a sip. "I want us all at the table—a nice family meal. That's a luxury that's rare enough already."

Jan thought there was an edge of reproach in her mom's tone. Her dad's mouth hardened into a line. He snapped on the little kitchen TV. "Market's up," he said. "A late rally this afternoon. Let's see how it turned out."

"Boys," her mom called, "wash your hands and come in to dinner. Use Josh's bathroom, not the downstairs one." She sighed. "Last time they washed up down here, the bathroom looked like a tornado went through."

"I tell Josh not to drop towels on the floor, but he forgets," Jan said.

"You're doing great, Jan. They're just all boy— that's to be expected." Her dad smiled at her.

"Yes," her mom said. "You are, Jan. It's a lot of responsibility and you're handling it fine. Not that being male is any excuse for making a mess."

"What's to eat?" Josh and Kevin came in and found their usual places.

"This is nice," Mrs. McIver said, "the whole family together. Nobody rushing off to a late meeting. Being together for a change."

Jan looked up at Connie Chung starting to announce the news.

Gram

July 18 was Gram's birthday. Mom swung by and picked up Jan and Josh after work. Dad was meeting them at the nursing home. Mom had stopped by the pastry shop to pick up the cake; Josh insisted on carrying the present, an electric lap robe. The circulation in Gram's legs was bad. She got cold even in the summer.

"We'll have a little party with Gram in her room and then stop for a bite on the way home." Mom handed Jan the cake box to hold. "Watch the flowers back there," she said to Josh. There was a pretty basket of carnations and roses on the back seat.

"Eat the cake first?" Josh sounded shocked. He was always wanting to do that, and nobody ever let him.

Mom laughed. "You can save yours for later, Josh.

I know you don't want to ruin your appetite." She started the car. "I wish we could do this in a more civilized way," she said to Jan. "Mapleview has such an early dinner hour and all."

"Gram's going to like the lap robe," Jan said. "And seeing everybody."

Jan's mom leaned out the window to adjust the mirror. She pushed a strand of hair back and gave Jan a wry smile. "I miss Mom, Jannie. You know? Sometimes I really miss her."

Startled for a second, Jan started to say, "But you see her almost every day." Then she sighed and said, "Yeah. Me, too."

Her mom backed the car into the street. "You know my grandmother lived with us, with Mom, for a long time? Until she died."

"What was your gram like?" Josh leaned over the seat. "When did she die?"

"A long time ago. I was ten."

Jan looked through the cellophane window in the box top at the pink and yellow roses on the cake. "Lucy's grandmother came and stayed when her mom got divorced. But Lucy said she kept bossing everybody around. Even Lucy's mom."

"I remember getting sick of tiptoeing around when my grandmother was sleeping. I know it used to get on Mom's nerves, having her always there."

"Still," Jan said, "the nursing home seems kind of gross. Sometimes it does, I mean. It's very nice and all."

Her mom patted her knee. "You don't have to pretend, Jan. It isn't all that great. Nobody wants to end up in one of those places. I know Mom didn't."

Funny, Jan thought, that there never were nursing homes on her soap. Jeff's parents, Reginald and Eugenia Lord, were as old as Gram. Reginald always had on a tweed jacket with one of those little scarves called ascots and Eugenia wore ropes of pearls and had a ripply laugh. They leaned on canes, but they looked and sounded fine. Gram's hands shook and her voice came in jerks, with gaspy breaths in between. Jan hadn't known that old ladies would get so they just farted out loud with people around. She hadn't expected that her gram could suddenly become so pitiful. Nobody told her. Her mom talked loud and acted cheerful when they visited. Jan didn't know where to look or what to say.

"Why don't we take her home?" Josh said. "She

could have the guest room. Or if Dad's using it, she could stay on my bottom bunk."

Jan's mom tightened her grip on the steering wheel. Jan shrank into the seat. "That's nice of you, Josh," her mom said after a minute. "But Gram needs lots of care, somebody with her, nurses and all that."

"Mapleview is pretty nice. They're taking good care of Gram." Jan tried to fill up the awful pause after what Josh had said. Why couldn't her mom ever talk about it? Just that one slip of Josh's and her mom was gripping the steering wheel and staring down the peaceful suburban street like she was afraid to miss a highway turnoff. Did she still love Jan's dad? Jan ached to ask. But that wasn't her mom's way. Her mom's way was to keep things in.

The nursing home was a long brick building like a motel. Just inside the door, Jan smelled the mix of Lysol and room deodorizer spray that was always her first impression of the place. Now, after their dinner, there was the warm food aroma that smelled like the cafeteria at school. It wasn't unpleasant, exactly, but had something in common with sweat. Once or twice in fourth period at school, before lunch, Janet had leaned sideways pretending to pick up something so she could sniff her armpit, making sure it wasn't her, smelling. Maybe it was cabbage. Cafeterias made a lot of vegetable soup with cabbage.

"Hi, Karen," the receptionist said to Jan's mom. "Lucille will be glad to see you guys."

"Do you know what sort of day she's having?" Since the stroke, Gram had been subject to mood swings. Sometimes she was withdrawn and sad, sometimes she was hostile and angry. Then you'd come back and she'd almost be her old self again—Gram.

"She's not acting out today," the receptionist said. "I think you'll find her much more appropriate than last time. She'll love the flowers and all."

Jan sighed. The nurses talked about Gram as if she were a naughty four year old. She and her mom and Josh walked the length of the corridor to the left. Gram's room was the last one. Jan tried not to peer into the rooms they passed, but she couldn't help herself. She had to look. An old man, so dried up he looked like a bug chrysalis, was lying with his skeleton of a body arced to accommodate a plastic tube down his throat. A woman with staring eyes was pulling, pulling aimlessly against the restraints holding her wrists to her bed. A bitter taste came into Jan's mouth. She swallowed and smelled the roses she was carrying.

"Happy birthday, Mom!" Jan's mom went in first, carrying the cake. She put it down on the bureau and kissed the stout white-haired woman hunched in the chair by the window.

"Pret-ty," Gram said, as Jan set the flowers on the window ledge beside her. "Jan-et. Josh." Her voice was deliberate, working for each syllable, with an intake of breath between. "Flow-ers."

Josh put the present on her bed. By the time Jan's mom had gotten the cake out and found some plates to serve it, her dad was there. They all clustered around Gram's chair and sang "Happy Birthday." Dad had brought the video camera and he filmed them singing and Gram smiling at the cake.

"Too man-y can-dles," Gram said. Jan knew she was pleased the whole family was there. Josh unwrapped the lap robe and shook it out over her knees. Dad plugged it in. They all ate cake and tried to say cheerful things.

They gave Gram birthday cards. Mom tacked them up on Gram's bulletin board after they read them to her. When they'd finished the cake, Josh got fidgety and it got harder to think of anything to say. Mom sent Josh out to the lounge to watch TV, but she and Dad and Janet didn't stay much after that anyway. "Have to get your beauty sleep," Dad said. "We don't want to tire you out."

Jan didn't want to leave. She kept feeling that somebody ought to say something, something besides just chitchat, but she couldn't think of anything.

"I love you, Mom," Jan's mom said, kissing Gram on the cheek.

"Have you smelled the roses, Gram?" Jan asked, holding the basket just under her chin. She held the bouquet under Gram's nose. The old woman took a deep breath. A naked expression came over her face, and she looked up at Jan, her eyes full of longing. Tears welled up in Jan's eyes. Jan leaned over and kissed Gram on the cheek. Gram's skin was light against her lips, fragile as old paper.

Jan put the arrangement back on the windowsill. Gram reached her hand toward her and Jan took it. They looked at each other and smiled, Gram's mouth lopsided now from the stroke. Did the flowers remind

Gram of her garden from years ago? Of bouquets Granddad had brought her when they were young?

Dad was cleaning up the wrappings, stuffing them into the trash. Mom was boxing the rest of the cake to leave for Gram to share with other people in the home. When they finished, everybody said good night and they all left.

"I hope she enjoyed that," Karen said to Jan as they pulled out of the parking lot. Josh was riding with Dad. They were going to meet at the Chinese restaurant.

"I think so. It's hard to know what she's thinking. She sure knew who we were tonight, though. Maybe she's getting better." Last time they'd visited, Gram had called Jan "Sally"—that was Gram's sister who died back in the forties.

"She's in and out. Tomorrow she may not even know me. That's the way she is now. They say it's little strokes."

"Well, you do a lot for her, Mom. And Dad does, too." Jan looked straight ahead, avoiding the searching glance she knew her mom would direct at her.

After a long pause Karen said, "It's not easy, Jan. Seeing her so helpless."

"Gram really loves you, Mom," Jan said. "She knows you're doing all kinds of things for her."

Her mom sighed. "Does she? I wonder." She shook her head and tried to laugh. "I don't usually go on like this, Jannie. I like to look at the bright side. Only, why can't life be like *The Cosby Show?* You know. It all looks so simple."

Jan sometimes watched Cosby reruns in her room at night. "Don't you love the kitchen they have? With the fireplace and the round table and all? The way they all joke around in there?"

Her mom laughed. "Yes. You just *knew* that in that kitchen nothing bad would happen. Or, if it did, it would get fixed in twenty minutes."

"Are you and Dad going to break up?" Jan just blurted that out. Out of nowhere. Her voice was so quiet she barely heard her own question.

Her mom waited before she answered. "I can't say for sure, Jan. Not now. I don't think so. We both want to work it out."

"I know he really does love you, Mom. I know—"

"Jannie, let's don't talk about it. OK? Ken and I agreed we wouldn't involve you or Josh. I know Dad's been a big help with Mom. You don't need to defend him. He took care of her house all those years. He's been like a son to her."

Jan wanted to keep talking, but she groped uncertainly for what to say. Their house was as warm and inviting as the Cosbys'. Jan's family had a gorgeous stone fireplace in the great room. They had one more bathroom than they even had people. Everything *looked* perfect. Then, why *wasn't* it? She remembered Dayton's furniture department in the mall.

"Why don't you and Dad redecorate the great room?" Jan suggested. "That would give you a common interest, like a hobby. I saw a great green leather sofa at the mall."

"We can't afford that now, Jannie. Maybe later. That lodge look is in now, though. I like it, too." Karen seemed relieved to change the subject. "The Parade of Homes this spring had a lovely cedar-shingle model featuring the Northwest style—lots of spruce and cranberry."

"Those colors would look perfect in there! You and Dad could have fun shopping for it all." Jan pictured the room, vivid and warm with lively colors, a fire glowing. "It would give you a feeling like Christmas all year."

Jan tried to hold on to the scenes of the family together in the redecorated room, the way she had at the store. But the images faded and questions crowded her mind. What kept people loving each other? Families from breaking apart? Suppose she and Steve went out for a while and found they really were in love? Eventually got married? What would keep them together, make their love last?

Was it flowers and intimate dinners? Little touches that let the other person know you cared? On *LBA*, Guy Woodruff had arranged a champagne brunch in a hot-air balloon floating high above Port Henry. Still, Jeff and Tricia and everybody else on the program had broken up and had affairs—lots of times—was that just human nature? Did people always want something new, get tired of the same old thing? Were relationships like furniture, then? Nobody liked old shabby things. Did that go for people, too? For relationships? Jan thought uneasily of Gram, and shifted in her seat.

"Josh and Dad got here first." Her mom pulled into

the restaurant parking lot. The other two were already inside and had taken a booth, where they were waiting. The waitress brought menus and Jan ordered her favorite, cashew chicken. The waitress left and Jan leaned back into the vinyl cushions, enjoying the way the high walls of the booth enclosed the four of them, her mom and dad on one side, Josh and her across from them.

"If it's pork," Josh asked, "how come it's called moo?" The others laughed.

"*Moo Shu* means pancakes, Josh, those steamed pancakes you like so much. It's a different kind of *moo.*" Karen spoke gently, seeing that Josh's feelings were hurt at their laughter.

"In China," Jan's dad said, "cows don't moo. That's English. In China, cows speak Chinese."

"So what do they say?" Josh grinned at his dad.

"That's a secret," Ken said. "You learn it when you learn Chinese. Along with how cats meow and dogs bark." Jan sipped her hot tea. Its fragrant warmth flooded her.

When they got in from dinner, the answering-machine message light was blinking. The nursing

home had called. Just after they had gone, Gram had
had another massive stroke. She was in the hospital, in
intensive care. Mom and Dad left again. "You stay,
Jan, and look after Josh. Go to bed. . . . That would
be the best thing," her mom called on the way out
the door.

"Do you suppose it was something . . ." Jan's voice
trailed off.

"No," her dad said. "Gram had a nice evening before this hit. She was with all of us."

"You're right," Mom said, her voice quivering. "I'm
glad she had that." Ken put his arm around her. Jan
saw her mom stiffen, then move closer to him. She
watched them leave. They were talking like Gram was
gone. But she'd had the other big stroke and gotten
over it.

"Will Gram die?" Josh sat down on the sofa, his
eyes wide. "I never knew anybody that died."

"Don't be dumb!" Jan snapped. "She's just had a
stroke, is all. They'll take care of it." The way Josh
looked fascinated, as if something amazing had happened, made Jan angry. Still, sinking down onto the
sofa cushions beside him, Jan didn't know what to feel
herself. The room looked different somehow; all the

detail leaped out at her sharp—the pictures on the wall, the shiny flecks in the gray stone of the fireplace. As if she were in a place she'd never been before. "Go put on your pj's, Josh," she said. "We ought to just act normal. That's what Mom said."

The next morning Jan went to the hospital with her mom. "They can't tell how she'll be until things have sorted themselves out," Karen said. "Right now Mom is on life support, a respirator and all. I have to warn you, it's not a pretty sight." There was a catch in her voice.

"It's OK," Jan said hastily. "I'll be all right." Riding up in the elevator, Jan stared at the fake wood-grain walls and watched the lights blink under the numbers. They went down the corridor to the left and into the section labeled "MEDICAL INTENSIVE CARE." There were four narrow beds with curtains on rods with rings like shower curtains. The end curtain was left open. The nurses' station was opposite the beds. Two nurses were there, filling in charts. One was big, with dark hair and a faint black mustache.

"Can I help you?" she said as they came up.

"Lucille Owens," her mom said. "We're here to see about Lucille Owens."

"Are you family?" The big nurse shoved a pencil behind her ear.

"I'm her daughter."

"She's stable," the nurse said. "No real change."

"Can we see her?"

"For five minutes every hour. One visitor."

"My daughter and I will just be a second."

The nurse was about to say, "No, only one visitor," when she looked at Jan's face. She nodded. "The lounge is down the hall. For families."

"Thank you." Her mom caught Jan's hand and guided her to the third cubicle. A wide plastic coil like a vacuum-cleaner tube was jammed into Gram's mouth. Her head was tilted back and her eyes were closed. Her hair was thin and uncombed, so she looked almost bald. Her hospital gown was pulled crooked, leaving one breast peeking out. Jan was stunned by the sight of one brown nipple poking through the slit. Gently, Mom reached over and adjusted the gown.

Gram had an IV in one arm and some kind of monitoring device strapped to the other one. And the breathing tube was hooked to a canister on the floor with a pump, going in and out. The rhythm of the pump horrified Jan. It just went on and on, no matter how awful Gram looked. No matter if her nipple was showing and she'd have died having people come around seeing her like that.

Jan gulped and held on to Mom. They stood together for a minute or two and then turned away. Her mom led her to the lounge and said they'd wait there until the doctor came through. "The doctors will probably set up a conference with the family sometime in the next two or three days. We'll have to decide . . ." Karen took a deep breath. "To decide how long to keep her like this."

"But what else . . . ?" Jan didn't want to know what her mom meant. She wanted to blot out the sight of Gram and her sad nipple showing and the plastic tubes and the dials and pumps.

Karen stared into space. "I guess you're never ready. I thought I was, but I'm not."

"Maybe Gram will be all right," Jan said. "I mean, she got over the other stroke pretty good." But this one was different. Jan knew that, but she didn't want to say it, even to herself.

They sat on the couch in the lounge waiting for the doctor. Doctors were always around on her show, Jan thought, as she thumbed through a magazine, too numb to notice anything but a blur of bright pictures. Here you waited and waited to talk to one. Jan leaned back against the vinyl sofa and closed her eyes. Doctors from her show—Dr. Terry Malone, Dr. Tricia Lord—those were the people she wished she'd see come through the door, shake hands with her mom.

On *Life Begins Again* nobody crammed ugly tubes in old ladies' mouths. In Central Hospital you could bet that nobody's gown would be pulled crooked in such a pathetic way. Families weren't left all alone to stare numbly at magazines. Nurses and doctors were there for them, pulling for them. That's what Jan felt she and her mom needed now.

Code Blue

At home later that day the phone rang. "Jan, it's for you."
Mom handed her the receiver. It was cordless and Jan
took it into the other room before she answered it. She
knew, just knew to the tips of her toes, that it had to
be Steve. At last. She'd been so dumb to think he
didn't like her. "Hello." She spoke in a low voice, not
wanting to sound nervous.

"Jan? You want to meet at the mall? Hang out for a
while?" It was Jess.

Jan swallowed. "Sure, Jess. Mom's home with Josh
and Kevin." After she hung up, Jan had second
thoughts. Was it OK to go out and have fun now? She
wasn't sure how she was supposed to act with Gram

like she was. "I could stay, Mom. Seriously, it's no big deal. If you need me here."

"No, Jannie. I'm OK. And it won't help Mom if you stay home all the time. Get out for a while. It'll be good for you."

"I thought I'd get Gram a card. At Hallmark's."

"That's a nice idea. She'll like that."

"For when she comes to," Jan said. "It'll be good if she has something to look at when she gets better."

Jan went out through the garage and picked up her bike. She pushed it out to the street. Candlewick Lane was a half-moon curve off Canterbury Drive. On Candlewick the houses were all brand new. Three or four had towers and round windows. Two were southern-mansion types with pillars and verandas. Then there were a few low ones, hugging the ground, with neatly clipped bushes under the windows. All of them had the same enormous garage door looming off the side. All of the houses were shut up tight with the shades drawn to keep the cool air in. Three houses down, two men from a lawn service were blowing grass clippings into a pile with a machine that worked like a vacuum cleaner in reverse, chasing the loose bits off the clean cement squares.

In their old neighborhood, in town, the houses on the block had more or less matched. Brick, with small front porches. The old block had seemed less lonely than these streets where the houses seemed to be trying to be so different from each other. Jan waved to the lawn-service guys, just for somebody to relate to in the stillness. They didn't wave back. Jan pedaled faster, letting the wind lift her hair off her forehead. At the mall she locked her bike to the rack and went in to meet Jess.

"My gram's really sick. She may not make it." Jan felt important telling Jess the news. Grief set her apart, made her special. Was that disgusting? Did it mean she was somehow *glad* Gram had had the stroke? Feelings were so complicated. There was one layer and then there was another one.

"I'm really sorry. What happened?"

Jan explained about the stroke. "She looked so awful. I couldn't believe it. Like everything that made her *her*—like all that was gone. She was just this *thing*—lying there."

Jess shuddered. "I'd die, seeing my grandmother like that. How did you stand it?"

"I knew how rotten Mom was feeling. I didn't want her to see I was so upset."

Jess nodded. "It must be awful for her. Jeez, what can you say?"

Jan shook her head. "Not much. I guess. But it's good to talk to somebody. Really." They went to Hallmark's and sorted through the racks in the get-well section.

"When you were little, did you used to make cards?" Jess laughed. "Draw pictures on the front and all?"

"Yeah. Those things looked awful. Folded lopsided, covered with paste."

"My mom's still got the ones I gave her," Jess said. "Moms are weird."

"You know, I almost wish I could make one for Gram. But I'm not sure what I'd say."

"And she might figure you were too cheap to buy one. Old people get funny sometimes."

None of the cards seemed just right. Jan finally picked one with pink roses on the front, like the ones in the bouquet they'd brought Gram. Inside, it just said something about feeling better. Tears burned

Jan's eyes, remembering the way Gram had looked, smelling the flowers.

She and Jess went to the food court for some pop. "Where's Amy?" Jan said. "I thought you guys always stuck together."

Jan shook her head. "We hang out a lot because we live next door to each other. I mean, we've known each other forever. Since nursery school. But Amy's so stuck on herself. Really." Jess was always intent on what was right. Sometimes Jan thought Jess sounded almost like a mom.

"She must have lots of friends." Jan took a long swallow of raspberry pop. "The way she looks and all."

"Yeah. You want to stay on her good side. School's so full of cliques. And she's so popular." Jess twisted a strand of her dark straight hair between her fingers. "Whatever she wants, she basically gets. My mom says she's spoiled rotten."

"How long's she been going with Keith?" Jan was bringing the talk around to boys gradually. She didn't want to flat-out ask Jess if she knew anything about Steve, if he was out of town or sick or something. She'd hate having Jess guess how she'd been waiting for Steve to call, watching for him when she rode her bike down the street, seeing him places where he probably wasn't just because she was dreaming about him half the time.

"You didn't hear?"

"Hear what?"

"How Amy and Keith broke up. A couple of weeks ago."

"No. She didn't say anything at tennis. What happened?"

Jess punched her ice with her straw. She looked uncomfortable. "I thought you knew. I thought somebody told you."

"Knew what?" Jan's voice wobbled.

"Amy's going out with Steve now. He really liked you first, you know. But she went after him."

"Oh," Jan said. Just "oh," like the air going out of a balloon.

"Like I said, Amy's really selfish," Jess said. "If you ask me, he's really dumb to fall for her act."

"I didn't know him all that well." Jan picked up her paper cup and held it in the palm of her hand, wanting the ice to burn against her skin, wanting another pain, *outside*, to focus on.

"He really liked you. Anybody could see that. If

you ask me, that's why she went after him. Just to prove something."

"It's no big deal," Jan said. "Like I said, I didn't know if I really liked him or not." She took a long swallow of her drink.

"Yeah, if you want my opinion, he'll be sorry," Jess said. "Amy is really fickle."

They sipped their drinks and looked around the court at the other tables. Weekdays were kind of quiet at the mall. "You'll think this is dumb," Jess said, looking embarrassed, "but I've got to watch what time it is. I don't want to miss my show. I forgot to set the tape."

"What do you watch?"

"*Life Begins Again.* It's on at two."

"You're *kidding*. That's my favorite. Isn't it the greatest?"

Jess smiled. "I never miss it. When school's on, Mom tapes it."

"I just started watching this summer. Who do you think is after Tricia Lord?"

"Hard to say. She's such a great person. She and Lorrie Babcock are my favorites on the show."

"I know. They are both so down-to-earth and

friendly. You'd never guess Tricia was a world-famous neurosurgeon. Besides being married to the head of a financial empire."

"Aren't you dying to see their son, JL? He's got to be incredible. A hunk beyond belief."

"He'll make Steve look sick." Jan laughed. There was a bitter edge to her laugh, but she speared some ice to suck and gave Jess a big smile.

"The best stuff on there has to do with Tricia and Lorrie. Did you know they used to be enemies?"

"No," Jan said. "It's hard sometimes, not knowing about what happened before this summer. That's weird. Why?"

"It was a long time ago. Before I started watching. Mom filled me in. Lorrie and Jeff were involved, like this thing he's been having with Charlotte, only more serious. Tricia suspected, but nobody could say if she knew for sure. Then Tricia got pregnant, and Jeff broke up with Lorrie. You know how important a son was to him. An heir to his empire and all."

"So how did they get to be friends after that?"

"Lorrie made up her mind to tell Tricia everything. She knew that Tricia's pride wouldn't let her stay with Jeff once she knew for real. Tricia was six months pregnant and completely unsuspecting when Lorrie dropped by the Lord mansion for tea."

"She told her, then? Lorrie let her know about her and Jeff?"

Jess shook her head. "She was about to. She was just on the edge of letting it all out when you'll never guess what happened."

"What?"

"The hurricane of the century struck. The roof blew off the mansion; they were trapped in the rubble without electricity or anything. Tricia was pinned under a massive beam. Then, guess what?"

"Tricia went into labor!"

Jess nodded. "And from that time on, Lorrie forgot all about Jeff. She worked night and day to save the mother and the baby."

"She's a real professional," Jan said. "You have to admire that."

"The next day, when Jeff broke through the debris and saved them, Lorrie just needed one look at his face to see it was all over between them. When he saw his son, that was it." Jess shook her head. "Wouldn't you love to have seen that show? So happy and sad both."

"And after that, Tricia and Lorrie became best friends," Jan said. "You're saying the whole experience made a bond between them."

"That's the way it was," Jess said. "It's sad, though, for Lorrie. Especially since she'll never have a baby herself."

"I know," Jan said. "Since she went over the waterfall in that canoe. I heard about that."

"And lost her own baby." Jess shook her head. "Tricia tried to save them both, she did everything, but it was hopeless."

Riding her bike home, Jan tried to keep thinking about *Life Begins Again,* but Steve and Amy blotted everything else out. Steve and Amy, Steve and Amy, a constant refrain in her head, humming with the sound of her bike tires. All those hours of waiting for Steve to call, all those days of seeing him at a distance, just knowing it was him. All those excuses she'd invented—his family was on a trip, he'd caught strep throat (there was a lot of it going around), he was kind of shy and was working up to phoning—all that left her feeling pathetic. Jan was right. Amy was disgusting. Really slimy. A phony friend.

At home, she dashed up to her room and switched on the TV. With the show in front of her, Jan finally blotted out the mocking chorus that had followed her home. Emma Martin and Lorrie Babcock were engaged in a race against time to prevent the assassin from striking yet again. After the menacing note delivered with the bouquet, Emma had assigned Lorrie the job of surveilling Tricia at the hospital while she and Mike accessed data from the Global Security Network on the computer.

Tricia had the day off because finally JL was flying in from his school in Switzerland so they could all be a family again. Tricia went in to the hospital, though, to pick up her messages. Lorrie went off the floor briefly to monitor a patient on eight. Seconds after Lorrie had disappeared, a suspicious figure appeared in the lounge across from Tricia's office: a tall blond man with a pockmarked face and teeth like a rat. Although he was wearing hospital greens, Jan knew as soon as she saw him, he didn't belong there. Instants later, a shot rang out. The crumpled body of Dr. Tricia Lord sank gracefully to the floor just outside her office, her red hair fanning out over her shoulders.

"Code Blue! Code Blue!" People in white coats with stethoscopes around their necks came flying down the hall with a steel gurney. Megan and Dawn rushed down from the desk.

"Shot? I don't believe it! Is she . . . ?" Lorrie Babcock clutched Dawn in stunned disbelief.

"Alive, but it's touch and go," Dr. Kevin Allen said. "Terry Malone is scrubbing. They are afraid there are serious cardiac implications."

"How are her vitals?" Lorrie was suddenly completely the professional. Even though it was her best friend at death's door.

"BP is way down, respiration weak, pulse thready."

"I'm to blame," Lorrie said. "I should never have left the floor. No matter what."

"You can't blame yourself, Lorrie," Emma said gently. "We're up against a real professional here. I've known that all along. It's in Terry's hands now. All we can do is pray."

"I'll scrub," Lorrie said. "Terry will need all the help he can get."

"Fan out and comb every inch of the area," Emma told the police who had rushed to the hospital. "He may have dropped the weapon, fleeing the scene."

While the commercials were on Jan went into the bathroom and splashed water on her face. JL would be on the show now for sure. And Jess was right— he had to be unbelievable. Steve would be pathetic beside him, Jan thought, grinding the towel against her face until it almost hurt. Jan imagined how she would feel if somebody had tried to murder her mom. How everybody would cluster around to offer support. How her dad and Josh would depend on her to be strong. "We have to remember, Mom's a real fighter," Jan imagined herself saying. "We have to hold good thoughts."

Sure enough, the first scene after the break introduced JL. The elevator door across from the nurses' station opened and a tall boy about sixteen, with wavy hair and dark eyes, got out.

"I'm looking for my mom," he told Dawn, behind the desk. "Do you know where Tricia Lord's office is?"

Dawn reached out and touched his arm. Jan could see that her heart really went out to him. "I'm afraid there's bad news," Dawn said.

Throughout the afternoon and into the night, JL, Jeff, and Emma waited for news from the OR. A bullet had lodged so close to the aorta that they had to fly in two specialists, one from Paris who was the best in the world. Even so, Tricia's life hung by a thread.

"I'll give it to you straight," Terry Malone told Jeff as he, JL, and Emma huddled together in the surgical lounge. "We could have massive bleeding."

"We could lose her? That's what you're saying?" Jeff was wild-eyed with grief.

"Mom's a fighter, Dad. We all know that." JL put his arm across his dad's shoulders.

"Right. If anybody can pull through this, Tricia can," Terry told them. "And she's got the best. Hold on to that."

Emma and Dawn went down to the cafeteria to get coffee for the men. "Times like these make you know what's really important," Dawn said. "All the Lord money and power are nothing now."

"What is there, in the end," Emma said philosophically, "but family and friends?"

A little after midnight, Tricia was brought from recovery to the ICU. The others stood helpless as Lorrie arranged Tricia's IV and placed the little bubble mask over her face to help her breathe. Tricia's lipstick was bright against her pale face. Her hair spread across the pillow.

"Mom never looked s-so beautiful," JL stammered, a catch in his voice.

"We'll find this madman, son," Jeff said. "I'll spare no expense, leave no stone unturned."

"You can believe that Mike and I will find this rat. And soon." Emma gathered up her belongings. "Tricia will make it. She has the best pulling for her." Emma left then, to get a few hours' sleep, leaving the two Lord men standing side by side, oblivious to everything but the slender woman in the bed in front of them fighting for her life.

Another World

In bed that night Jan lay rigid, wide awake. Amy Metz, with her three-hole pierced ears and her frizzy hair and her innocent laugh, was a fake through and through. And Steve was a pathetic wimp not to see through her. He'd live to regret blowing off Jan for somebody as phony and shallow as that. Men were so dumb. Look at her dad and Allyson. Allyson and Amy. A pair, for sure. Look how Jess saw right through Amy Metz's act. And she was right, too, Jan told herself, thumping her lumpy pillow, Steve Hauser would be sorry someday. Her dad had been fascinated by that floozy Allyson, until he had had to chose. Then he'd known her mom was worth a hundred of her. Jess had Amy

Metz pegged. Amy was a show-off; she only cared about herself. Steve would see how wrong he'd been.

Imagine if she had a new boyfriend, like JL. Jan would give everything just for the chance to walk past those two—Amy and Steve—just casually holding JL's hand. JL was the greatest-looking guy she'd ever seen. And so sensitive. Jan's heart went out to him, so alone there with Jeff at the end of the show. Jan thought how wonderful it would be to go to Port Henry, to help Emma find the assassin and to be there for JL. People on the show said that all the time, "I'll be there for you." It was touching the way they cared. Jan stretched out under the sheet and saw herself coming up to Emma, offering to help.

"Welcome to Port Henry, Jan." Emma Martin shook the gorgeous, rippling waves of hair out of her face and smiled. "Are you ready to try life out on the edge?"

Jan couldn't believe how incredible Emma looked up close. It must have taken hours to get her mascara layered like that, and her glossy lips were fire-engine red. Emma's hair was what really struck a person, though—unbelievably long and glossy and curled so perfectly you couldn't imagine how much time she must have spent with a curling iron to get it that way.

"Fill me in on the details," Jan said.

"The gun was a standard make," Emma told Jan. "This man is too smart to leave obvious clues."

"He has to be a professional."

Emma nodded. "Whoever is behind this is deadly serious. We have to find him and we have to do it before it's too late."

"Where are you thinking of plugging me in?"

"I want you to work in my office, with JL. He needs all the support he can get. I can tell you'll be there for him."

Jan nodded. "I'll do what I can. Will Tricia make it?"

"She's a fighter. We all know that. And she's got the best—that counts for a lot."

"Yeah. Terry Malone is tops, plus the French specialist. And Lorrie Babcock is a professional through and through. If anybody can pull Tricia through, they can."

"They don't come any better than Lorrie," Emma said, leaning toward Jan earnestly. Then Emma looked up. They were sitting in the hospital cafeteria opposite the elevator. "Speak of the devil," Emma said playfully as the doors slid open. Lorrie came toward them, unmistakable with her shimmering platinum cropped hair and her enormous warm brown eyes.

"You know we're grateful for your help, Jan." Lorrie had such a sensitive face, her eyes misted as she expressed her thanks when Emma explained Jan's presence. "We have to get to the bottom of this. And quickly."

"Between you and I," Emma said, lowering her voice to a whisper, "I believe another attempt will be made soon."

"But she's here in Central! Surrounded by family and friends. Guarded by the best." Jan had to think Emma was being overcautious.

"There's nothing like family," Lorrie said, musingly. "No matter how much money and power you have, in the end it's family that counts."

"You must really care about JL," Jan said. "Since he wouldn't be alive today without you."

Lorrie smiled. "He calls me Aunt Lorrie. I've almost been another mother to him. And he's a very special young man. Wait until you meet him."

"And that will be soon," Emma said, finishing her coffee and standing up. "I'll take you over to my office.

JL will be there any minute. The two of you can use the computer to check the records of all the new hires at Central for the past three months. Get a list and then call up their resumes. Look for anything suspicious. I'll fill you in on the way over."

In less than half an hour Jan found herself in the office Emma shared with her partner, Mike, in their work as private eyes. She was working side by side with JL Lord. Jan could hardly believe that this amazingly good-looking boy, heir to the entire Lord empire, was as sweet and down-to-earth as Lorrie had said.

"Emma says we'll know a suspicious resume when we see it. Emma says you develop a sixth sense. Suddenly something jumps out at you."

JL laughed bitterly. "I wish this guy would jump out. I'd love to get my fingers around his throat."

The two of them stood side by side, scrolling through resume after resume. "Look at this, JL!" Jan scrolled back just as JL was going on to the sixteenth file. "I think we may have found our man!"

Their hands touched as they leaned over the keyboard. It was almost as if an electric current had run between them. "I see what you mean," JL said, his voice rippling with excitement. "It's too perfect. Most of the others have a mistake here and there. And every single month's accounted for. Real people's lives aren't that neat."

Leonard White was the name on the file. He was an orderly assigned to ferry patients to and from the OR and X-ray. "With his job he has access to the whole hospital, Jan!" JL's voice shook. "I think you've found him!"

"Wouldn't they check references? If he'd put phony ones, wouldn't they have found out?"

JL frowned. "Not if he went one step farther. Suppose he had a partner? Somebody who helped him fake it?"

"He's not working alone." Jan's blood froze at the thought. "A hired killer." They called the first reference, the Shady Rest Nursing Home. The phone rang and rang. Then a man came on, "Hello? Hello?" He sounded puzzled.

"Who am I calling, please?" Jan hadn't thought through just what to say.

"I don't know who you're calling, lady. But what you've got is a pay phone. Over by the docks." The man clicked off.

JL's eyes blazed with fury. "We have to get to the hospital. And stop Leonard White from coming near my mom." They dashed out of Emma's office.

JL's emerald-green sports car with ivory-leather bucket seats darted through Port Henry's traffic, leaving a trail of blowing horns. "I'll kill him, Jan. If that man has laid a finger on my mom, I'll kill him with my bare hands." They turned into the Central Hospital parking area, gravel spewing behind the wheels as they raced against the clock to save an innocent woman.

Cardiac ICU was on two. As soon as she and JL stepped off the elevator, Jan knew it was too late. The nurse's station was deserted. The air crackled with suspense. Both of them knew, even before they rounded the corner and saw the knot of professionals feverishly working over Tricia, that the killer had, incredibly, struck again.

"What happened?" JL went white as a sheet.

"Take it easy, son." JL was about to burst into the inner room where the team was clustered around Tricia, but Jeff put his hand on JL's elbow, restraining him. "Let them work. Don't go in now."

"Is Mom . . . ?"

"She's alive. Barely." There was an undertone of fury in Jeff's voice. "The respirator was tampered with. Terry discovered it when he came to check on her. If he hadn't come in when he did . . ." Jeff swallowed hard.

"But an alarm goes off if somebody stops breathing in ICU." Jan had learned that the first week she watched the show.

"The back-up systems were disconnected as well. It definitely looks like an inside job by a professional." Jeff's jaw was clenched. The man was clearly on the edge of collapse. "We've called the police, of course. And Emma. They should be here any minute."

Jan felt a huge lump in her throat. It was all so unfair. They'd been through so much already.

"Dad, did you see an orderly? Did somebody bring Mom back from X-ray?"

"Blond guy," Jeff said. "I saw him at a distance. You think it was him? I'll kill him." Jeff's face convulsed with pain and rage.

"Which way did he go?" Jan's voice was crisp and even. Horrible as the situation was, she held together like a professional.

Jeff gestured toward the OR wing. "That way. But

you can't. . . . Wait. . . . The police . . ." His voice faded behind them as Jan and JL dashed down the corridor in the direction of the killer.

"Dad's right, Jan. This could be dangerous. Let me go." JL put his hand on her arm. Jan shook it off.

"This is my fight too, JL. With Tricia's killer loose, none of us is safe." They slowed down as they came to the swinging doors in the OR corridor. Cautiously, Jan pushed one open. The hall was deserted and dimly lit. Jan remembered that Central rotated its surgery schedule. Cardiac wasn't usually scheduled on Wednesdays—only emergencies were covered then.

Jan was about to say, "Nobody's here, JL. Let's go back." Then they heard a metallic sound, a light banging noise. "He's clearing out his locker," she whispered, recognizing the sound at once. How many times had she slapped hers shut and dashed off to class, that exact sound echoing behind her? "The rat is about to take off for good."

The locker room was at the end of the corridor on the left. They crept to the door, their rubber-soled shoes making no noise on the linoleum. Cautiously, they peered around the door frame. The man was alone, standing on a chair and reaching up to the ceiling panel above him, prying the square tile off. The gun sparkled silver in the shaft of sunlight from the window behind him as it dropped into his waiting palm. If he turned his head, he would see them. Jan grabbed JL's wrist and pulled him back. They flattened themselves against the wall and waited.

"I'm out of here," the man muttered. "It's goodbye, Lenny." Seconds later he rushed past them, never glancing in their direction. They waited until he was out of sight. Then, terrified they might lose him, they dashed in pursuit.

Jan and JL had no time to call for help, only time to plunge through the stairway door just past the OR entrance and follow the thud of his footsteps to the first floor and the parking lot. Outside, the sun momentarily blinded Jan. But she heard an engine being revved. Grabbing her arm, JL raced for his car. They barely had time to get to the street as Leonard White's rusty junker disappeared around the corner. JL was after him like a shot.

Jan leaned back into the luxurious leather seat of JL's sports car. For a second, she closed her eyes, only to snap them open instantly. Jan had seen again the silver flash of the revolver dropping from the ceiling into White's outstretched hand. That is an image, Jan thought, that I may never erase.

The car ahead turned onto a highway entrance. Where was he leading them? JL maneuvered to the right lane and clicked his turn signal. "Where's this creep going?" he muttered. In the fast-moving highway traffic, JL was careful to drop back several cars behind White's.

"My guess is he's not working alone," Jan said. "He's meeting someone."

JL nodded. "He smells like a hired gun. But who could be behind him, Jan? Who?"

Jan shook her head. "Tricia has no enemies. How could she? There is a mystery here, some missing piece we aren't seeing."

Skillfully maneuvering the low-slung sports car with one hand, JL reached out to Jan with the other and enclosed her hand in his. "They say something good comes out of even the worst times. Meeting you, Jan, is one of the best things that ever happened to me."

"I feel I've known you all my life," Jan told him. "We can't have just met."

Up ahead, Leonard White turned on his blinker.

He was heading for a country road. JL eased up on the gas and signaled a turn. "He must have a mountain cabin up here somewhere—a hideout." JL followed the rusty sedan up the twisting mountain road.

"Dad has a place up here," JL said. "He doesn't use it anymore. Back when I was a kid, we'd come and fish weekends."

"How come he and Tricia don't use it more?"

JL looked uncomfortable. "Mom always hated the place. I don't know for sure, but I think maybe Dad brought another woman there. Mom connected it to a time in their relationship she wanted to forget."

They were up quite high, the air was cool. Jan heard the sound of rushing water ahead. "Bridal Veil Falls," JL said.

"What?"

"I remember now." They came around a granite cliff and saw the falls directly in front of them, a long narrow splash of foam cascading down the mountainside. "That's how Dad used to tell me to find our cabin. 'Count the turnoffs,' he'd tell me. 'We're the third turnoff after Bridal Veil Falls.' Funny how stuff like that comes back to you. I haven't been up here since I was eight."

"It's weird that Leonard White is going to the same area." But barely had Jan spoken, when things got even stranger. Leonard White, up ahead, flashed his blinker again.

"Jan." JL's voice was icy cold. "He's taking the third turnoff after the falls. Leonard White is heading for my dad's cabin!"

The Spotted Lily

Neither Jan nor JL knew what to say. For a wild moment, Jan asked herself, Is it possible? Could Jeff be behind this? Immediately she rejected the thought. Nobody could fake the emotion that the powerful executive displayed at his wife's bedside.

JL pulled off behind some trees beside the road.

"We'll go in on foot?" Jan asked. She climbed out of the car and stood under the tall pines that loomed up, almost sinister, above her and JL.

JL nodded. "Let's go through the woods and watch the cabin from the trees. See if White's alone."

The ground was thick with pine needles and dotted with clumps of fern. Circling a large boulder, Jan came upon a sight that made her skin prickle: a patch of pale green lilies, lilies with black speckles. They matched the mysterious flowers that someone had sent to Tricia. A chill ran through her. She knew now, for sure, they were about to find the killer.

At the edge of the woods they huddled behind a big tree and looked out at the log chalet with a big deck wrapped around two sides. Leonard White came out of the side door and crossed the deck. His feet crunched on the gravel driveway. They held their breaths and pressed in closer against the tree trunk. White went to the passenger side of his car and reached in for a bag on the front seat.

High above Jan and JL, a squirrel dislodged a chunk of rotten wood. A cloud of dust particles followed it to the ground. Jan held her breath and swallowed desperately. Then she sneezed. When she opened her eyes, Jan was looking directly at the menacing features of Leonard White. A scar streaked down the right side of his face.

"This is private property. Youse kids don't belong here."

"We were hiking," JL said. "We didn't mean to bother you."

"Get outta here," White snarled.

"Sure," JL said, "no problem. We're just leaving."

"Sorry to bother you," Jan said. The chalet door slammed. Jan and JL looked across. A woman was coming down the steps to the driveway, the sun sparkling on her close-cropped platinum hair. Jan felt all the air go out of her, as if someone had kicked her in the stomach. JL went white as a ghost. They should have run, but they stood, rooted to the ground.

"What's going on, Lenny?" Lorrie Babcock called. "I thought you just came to pick up your . . ." She stopped. "Jan! JL! Oh my God!"

"Aunt Lorrie!" JL sounded as if the words were being torn from his throat. "You were Mom's best friend."

"You were like s-sisters," Jan stammered. "Closer than sisters. How can it be true . . . ?"

"Jeff and I belong together," Lorrie said. "There's never really been anybody else for me. Underneath he feels the same way. He has to. It's sad what happened to Tricia, but there was no other way."

"You almost killed her. Do you think her husband will thank you for that?" Jan was so angry, felt so betrayed, she hardly knew what she was saying.

"*Almost?*" Lorrie spun around toward Leonard

White. "Lenny, I unhooked the alarm system. You were going to take care of the respirator. Lenny, have you screwed up again?" Lorrie's body was rigid with rage. "Tricia is still *alive?*"

"Is it my fault that Malone guy wandered in at the wrong time? Could I have predicted that?"

A strange calm seized Lorrie. "I'll do it myself. I should have taken care of it in the first place. Now you'll have to take care of these two. They cannot go back to Port Henry. You understand, Lenny?"

"Keep Jan out of this," JL pleaded. "Let her go."

"Lorrie, it's not too late," Jan begged. "You aren't a murderer, Lorrie. You can still save yourself."

"Jeff loved me. He called me his spotted lily. Because of my freckles." Lorrie touched her cheek and giggled. Jan's blood ran cold. "Nothing will ever separate us again." She turned and looked straight at Jan. Gazing into the brown eyes of Lorrie Babcock, Jan saw madness looking back at her. Lorrie Babcock was insane. At that moment, Jan abandoned all hope.

Lorrie drove off. "I'll kill you two when it gets dark," Leonard White said. "Fewer snoops after dark. You kids mind waiting?" He wheezed a laugh. Jan shuddered.

Leonard White herded them into the house, his gun aimed at their backs. He gestured for them to go into a storage room behind the kitchen. Jan heard the bolt slide into place and his footsteps disappear into another room. There were no windows, no other exits. The room was as black as her despair. The only comfort was JL's arm around her, pulling her close.

"Jan, we're incredibly lucky," he whispered.

"What do you mean?" Was JL as mad as Lorrie Babcock?

"He's locked us in the utility room."

"What's so great about that?" Jan could just make out the shape of the furnace behind them. The room smelled of pine boards.

"There's a trap door."

"What? Where?"

"Dad had it put here for access under the house to check on pipes freezing, that sort of thing." JL led her behind the furnace. Jan heard him grope for the rope circle that served as a handle. He had to tug with both hands—the door obviously had not been used for a long time and the hinges were stiff. It creaked open. Below was a ladder down through the maze of supports under the house. The house was resting on pillars where it extended out from the hillside. The afternoon sun beamed between the wide-spaced boards of the deck and made bright stripes on the ground below them.

In minutes, they were gone. Silent as smoke, they faded back into the trees. Fast as the wind, they dashed for JL's car. Back on the road, desperately chasing Lorrie Babcock, Jan and JL couldn't pause to register the terrible danger they had just escaped. They had no time to be afraid for themselves. All their thoughts were on Tricia. In an hour they'd be at Central. Jan prayed that Lorrie would not have struck again.

When the elevator door slid open and JL and Jan staggered out, who should be right in front of them, by the nurse's station, but Jeff?

"*Son!* We've been beside ourselves with worry. Where have you two been?"

"Mom . . . is she?"

"Relax. Tricia is in the best of hands. Lorrie's in there with her now."

JL made a strangled sound, half rage, half despair, and took off down the hall, Jan right beside him.

Bewildered, Jeff followed, calling, "JL! Stop! This is a *hospital!*" They arrived at the ICU just as Lorrie Babcock was standing beside Tricia's bed about to give an injection.

"*No!*" Jan shrieked. She dashed through the outer room and into Tricia's cubicle. She knocked the syringe out of the astonished Lorrie Babcock's hands. Lorrie's face turned ashen as she looked at the two of them.

"How . . . ?" Lorrie's word was like a whimper. Jan almost felt sorry for her, her whole world crashing around her at that moment.

"Jan? What's going on?" Jeff was sputtering in bewilderment.

"She's the one, Dad. Lorrie's been trying to kill Mom."

"I don't believe it." The voice from the bed startled Jan and JL. Tricia was conscious.

At that moment Emma Martin burst in, summoned by a nurse who had seen Jan and JL's headlong dash for the ICU. "What's happening?" she demanded.

"I think Jan has lost her mind," Jeff said. "She knocked the syringe out of Lorrie's hands when she was trying to give Tricia a sedative." He pointed to the needle lying on the carpet. Emma picked it up and sniffed it. Her face stiffened.

"A few drops of this and nothing would have saved Tricia. This is a rare poison that leaves no trace in the human body. Jan and JL have saved Tricia's life."

After Lorrie had been taken downtown to be booked, Jan, JL, Emma, and her boyfriend, Dr. Sean Spencer, chief of psychiatry, sat in the cafeteria and talked about the incredible drama that had just unfolded.

"Lorrie knew all my plans," Emma moaned. "It's all my fault. I put you at great risk, Jan. I should have never let you and JL work on your own. I'll never forgive myself."

"You can't blame yourself," Sean said, comfortingly. "If anybody should have caught on to Lorrie, I should. I worked with her every day. I can't believe I never noticed . . ."

"No one could have guessed," Jan said. "She was too clever."

"How could she have been so warm and caring and, underneath, a cold-blooded killer?" JL shook his head in bewilderment.

"I think Lorrie Babcock was not one person," Sean said, "but two. The genuine caring woman we all loved, and a sociopath torn apart by jealousy. The loss of her baby must have triggered the split and allowed the alternate personality to emerge."

"I feel sorry for her," Jan said. "She seemed so lost."

"You're amazing, Jan. She tried to kill you and you feel sorry for her." There was no mistaking the glow in JL's eyes as he smiled at Jan. She blushed.

"Sometimes it takes something like this," Sean said, "just to make us remember how lucky we all are."

"And what's really important," JL added. "Mom and Dad and I have never been closer. We are a real family now."

Jan's eyes misted up. "Well, all's well that ends well," she said to lighten the mood. The others laughed and agreed.

*   *   *

In Jan's room in Forest Grove, the ceiling fan made a breeze that fluttered a Kleenex off her bedside table to the carpet. Outside, dimly audible through the closed windows, a dog barked. Jan turned onto her side and murmured incoherently.

A Mission

Gram came off the respirator on Thursday and was moved to a regular room. She wasn't conscious, but she groaned sometimes and sort of jabbered. Jan and her family just stood and looked at her. They took her hand and stroked her cheek, but Gram didn't know. The doctors couldn't say if she would get better or not. "Time will tell," one of them said.

Jan's mom looked exhausted. Her dad tried to get her to rest. He brought Karen flowers. "I thought you needed these more than Lucille," he said. "Something pretty to brighten your day."

Her mom smiled, but Jan saw it was forced. "Thanks, Ken," she said, "that was thoughtful." But Karen didn't move to kiss him on the cheek or put her arm around him the way she would have before their problems with Allyson.

Jan couldn't stand floating in this fog. Why couldn't they fly in experts, Jan thought, to operate on Gram? Was Gram getting better? Dying? Or just lying there, always the same? And what about her mom and dad? Did they love each other? Would they stay together or not? What was the truth of it? That's what Jan wanted to know, just the simple truth.

Jan flashed back to the dream where she had swung the stringless racket futilely as the ball whizzed through it. No wonder she had dreams like that if she lived in a world where nobody ever got to the bottom of things. A world where people just went on and on and on, not knowing how it would all come out. In Port Henry, she and JL had solved the mystery and saved Tricia. Lorrie had been behind it all. Painful as that was, they had all faced her treachery and had gotten on with their lives.

"Why can't they *do* something?" Jan muttered in disgust. "Can't we get some specialists in? Aren't there neurosurgeons that fix strokes?"

Her mom sighed. "I wish. I wish we had Mom back.

I can't believe I complained about visiting her. I'd give anything . . ." She was sobbing.

Her dad frowned. "You did everything, Karen." He put his hand on her shoulder, touching her gently. He turned to Jan. "Some things aren't fixable. We just have to live with that."

But Jan wasn't ready to take that view.

The key was Allyson. Her mom needed to face that woman, hear her ask for forgiveness. Hear how she'd come on to Jan's dad during a difficult time in her parents' relationship. Her mom and dad didn't need these tiresome exercises from a therapist, these endless weeks of strain and apology and weak smiles. One big scene would clear the air, Jan knew. And Allyson owed them that. Allyson needed to know, too, that her dad had just turned to her in a weak moment. That it meant nothing. That for her dad, family was all that mattered.

Jan leaned against the wall in Gram's hospital room and watched her mom standing beside the bed, her cheeks pale and her eyes teary. And her dad, frowning in frustration at not getting through to her. Jan ran her palm against the smooth wall behind her.

She bopped her hand back and forth against the hard surface.

Jess had told her about Lorrie's going to confront Tricia. Allyson had been at the party her parents had gone to the night Jan heard them fighting. If only her mom had marched across the room and stood there, with Jan's dad on her arm. Allyson would have wilted. Her mom could have said, "All right, Ken, here we both are: the two women in your life. The time has come to make a choice. It's Allyson or me."

Jan looked at her mom's tense face and thrilled at the thought that Karen might have risked everything that way. That her mom would be willing to have her marriage go up in flames if Ken made the other choice. Janet knew that, at that moment, her dad would discover his true feelings. Jan knew that, underneath, her parents truly loved each other.

But Jan's mom had just hidden on the other side of the room and never said boo to Allyson, the home wrecker. Then she'd come home and yelled at Jan's dad. Jan tapped her fingers against the smooth wall behind her. *She* could confront Allyson. Make that woman crawl.

Jan tried to think logically about how she might

look for Allyson. All she had was a first name and a place, her dad's life insurance company downtown. Jan had been there, of course, but it was a big building. How could she find one woman with so little to go on? How would Emma Martin think, if she were in this spot?

Jan had a feeling she'd know Allyson on sight. She closed her eyes and pictured her for the five hundredth time. Big hair. With those kinds of rat's-nest snarls that some women thought were sexy. Blond (her mom had said that). Jan thought she probably had big brown hound-dog eyes (which showed that her hair was most likely dyed). Big breasts that jiggled under her flame-pink jersey shirt. A black miniskirt. Boots, even though it was summer. Or maybe those strappy sandals that wrapped around her ankles.

Jan was so sure, in fact, that she would recognize Allyson that she first considered hiding in the lobby of the building, surveilling, until she spotted her. She could loiter over by the newsstand, pretend to read *Newsweek*. Then, seeing the woman swish through the revolving doors, wiggling her butt all the way over to the elevators, Jan would simply step over to her. "Excuse me, aren't you Allyson?"

"How did you know?" the woman would say. After that, Jan's plans were a little blurry. She hadn't figured out exactly what she'd say to her. But, distinct as anything, she could see Allyson's reaction to what Jan told her about her mom and dad and how they really loved each other and always would. Allyson's mascara would run and streak as she wept quietly in her corner of the booth at the coffee shop off the lobby, where Jan had taken her.

"I hated you, Jan," Allyson would say, between sobs. "I hated the hold all of you had on Ken."

"Maybe you were in some sense a victim yourself, Allyson," Jan found herself saying. She felt almost sorry for the smear-faced woman, blotting her raccoon eyes with a tissue. "It hasn't been easy for any of us." Like Lorrie, Jan thought, Allyson was pathetic more than she was evil.

To be practical, Jan decided she'd better try to find out Allyson's last name and her office number. Her dad, she knew, had a directory of people in the company. She'd seen it on his desk in the study. Jan went in there the next time she was alone in the house with Josh and Kevin. Poring over the directory, she found Allyson Larson, an underwriter. She was on three.

That was two floors down from her dad, the way he'd said. Jan wrote down the office number.

On Monday Kevin and Josh were going to overnight soccer camp for two days. Jan could catch the train into town in the morning, and then the bus to the office building. She knew which bus because she'd taken it with her dad. Even when they had lived in the city, her parents had never let her go downtown by herself. Now, though, Jan was going. No matter what.

Jan put her ticket under the clip on the back of the seat in front for the conductor to punch. She looked out the window. Once it left the station, the train ran along behind the suburban towns, past run-down brick warehouses and boarded-up factories. The sun beat down on three rusty freight cars at a railroad siding; the doors of the cars were open and Jan stared out the window into the dark, empty space. Her train pulled alongside a tall fence that partly hid piles of rusty junker cars, some of them smashed from wrecks. There were so many of them. Jan tried not to imagine the shards of broken glass, the mangled bodies. Her hands were sweaty and cold.

Jan looked at a clump of stubby brick apartment buildings with fire escapes zigzagging up the backs. Trash was blowing around behind them, and there were big bare spots with no grass. Some kids Josh's age were playing, walking along the tracks as if they were on a tightrope, arms out stiff, swaying, trying to keep on the rail. Jan thought of the mall, of Candlewick Lane with its lawn sprinklers and tight shut blinds. It was the same world, but you could hardly believe it. Suppose she lived in one of those buildings, with the wash hanging on the porch and the trains going past? Everybody would see your underwear, she thought. Even your bras.

She thought of their old neighborhood, not run-down and junky like this one, but not shiny and new like Forest Grove, either. On a train, you noticed how there were so many different kinds of places, all side by side. Driving in a car, the way she'd always gone into town from Forest Grove, Jan mostly saw the highway with its green signs and fences and steep banks along the sides. She and her mom listened to tapes. Going in the car, she didn't see beat-up, junky buildings or children playing in bare dirt back yards.

In the car, Jan whooshed from home to downtown and skipped the worlds that lay in between.

The train swayed, picking up speed between stations. "Glen Harbor is next! Glen Harbor." The speakers were staticky and hard to understand. She couldn't possibly miss her stop—Central Station, the last one. Still, they made her nervous, the constant announcements that she kept struggling to figure out. At each station the doors hissed open and a few shoppers straggled on. It was 9:30. The commuter crowds were long gone.

Jan glanced around at the other people on the train. A few smartly dressed women in linen suits and silk shirt dresses, going into town for shopping and lunch. Some teenagers in jeans and T-shirts, probably going into the city just to hang out. Jan stared down at her fingers, folded carefully in her lap.

Jan followed the crowd when the train pulled into the downtown station. She went up a flight of cement steps, littered with trash, and came out onto the bustling city street. There was a newspaper/magazine stand on the corner, and a flower stall next to that. The sidewalk was full of people hurrying. Jan hurried, too, around the corner and down the block, over to the bus shelter where she could catch the number 11 to her dad's office.

Allyson Larson's office was 306, which meant that Jan shouldn't run into her dad. Especially since she'd heard him tell her mom he'd be in meetings all morning. "In the conference room on six. Buzz me there directly, if something comes up," he'd said. It was almost as if fate were helping her, clearing her path to Allyson. Still, Jan ran the dollar bill through her fingers nervously, waiting for the bus.

What was she going to say when she finally came face to face with Allyson? "I have something important to discuss. Could we go somewhere quiet? This is very personal." She could say that, in a dignified tone. Allyson would immediately be alerted that Jan was not a person to trifle with. When they sat down in a booth in the coffee shop, Jan would say, simply, "My name is Janet McIver. I believe you know my father?"

Shock and disbelief would be written across Allyson's face. "Oh n-no," she would stammer, "not his daughter."

The bus rumbled to the curb. Jan smoothed down her hair and licked her lips. Her throat was dry. It was a short ride to the building. At the gold revolving door, Jan hesitated for a moment. Then she stepped up, put out her palm, and pushed, whirling herself into the dim marble lobby. A big directory was on the wall opposite the door, and a blue-uniformed guard sat under it, reading a magazine. The shiny brass elevators gleamed off to the right. Jan scurried toward them. She pushed *up* and, then, when the doors opened and let her in, *3.*

The elevator let her out into a big open area where people were sitting at computer terminals. The outer walls were lined with cubicle offices with numbers on the doors. One of those was Allyson Larson's. Jan looked around her, disoriented.

"Can I help you, hon?" A young woman in a knit suit was sitting behind a desk facing the elevator.

"I'm looking for Allyson Larson," Jan said, her voice squeaking in a way that surprised her. She should have looked for a ladies' room first. Suddenly she needed to go to the bathroom.

"Over there." The woman pointed. "Three-oh-six. She expecting you? You must be Ali." The woman smiled.

Jan nodded quickly.

The door to Allyson Larson's office was open. A woman was sitting at the desk, but it clearly wasn't her. Jan was almost relieved, seeing the plain, rather chunky-looking woman with hair the color of under-cooked toast, sitting reading a stack of papers.

"Where's Allyson Larson?" she asked, startled out of her planned dialogue.

"Huh?" The woman looked at her blankly, pre-occupied with her papers. Her eyes were pale blue, the color of faded denim, and her hair was cut in two wings that looped halfway down over her ears. She was wearing big out-of-style plastic glasses. "You're look-ing for me?"

"I was looking for Allyson Larson."

"That's me. What can I do for you?" The woman looked mildly annoyed. "You aren't selling Girl Scout cookies or something? I'd like to help, but we don't allow people selling things in the office."

"No." Jan swallowed, looking for the next thing to say. "No. I just wanted to meet you."

Allyson Larson frowned. "Meet me? Why? Are you one of Ali's friends? Have you got a problem? You look upset."

Jan was standing in front of a chair just inside the

door. Suddenly her knees gave out and she sat in it. "I'm Jan," she said, "Janet McIver."

The woman came around from behind the desk. "Ken's little girl?"

"You know my dad?" Jan had meant that to sound sarcastic, but it came out a pitiful wail. Tears welled up in her eyes and spilled over. Allyson handed her a tissue.

"Yes," she said. "I know him. What do you want, Jan? Why did you come?"

"I wanted to see you. To tell you to leave my dad alone," she blurted out, her eyes squeezed almost shut.

"Who told you . . . ? Ken doesn't know . . . ? No, of course not." Allyson closed her office door. "Wipe your eyes, Jan, and blow your nose. Then let's go down to the coffee shop where we can talk."

"I don't know what you want from me, Jan." Allyson said, stirring her coffee. "Why did you want to see me?" She tore open another sugar packet and poured it into her cup. Jan watched her, stunned. Allyson must be pushing a hundred forty pounds and she just dumped in sugar without a second thought.

Allyson Larson was wearing a white polyester blouse with a crumpled bib of ruffles down the front, a gray skirt, and not even any lip gloss as far as Jan could see. Dress moccasin shoes that didn't do anything to make her calves look less bulging. "I don't understand what happened," Jan said, playing with the wrapper of her straw. "Why did Dad . . . ?" Her voice trailed off.

"You were expecting a bimbo, right?" Allyson smiled. "A floozy in a tight dress and three-inch heels?"

"N-no," Jan stammered. "I wasn't at all. Really." She tried not to stare at Allyson's broad bland face across from her. Could this woman have been swept away by passion? Wearing moccasins and giant plastic frames that slid partway down her nose? Jan took a swallow of Coke to cover her confusion.

Allyson frowned. She bit her lip. "Look. I don't know what to say to you, Jan. I don't want to make light of this, and please excuse me if you thought I was laughing at you." Allyson lifted her coffee cup and held it halfway to her mouth, gazing off into the distance, over Jan's head. She took a sip and put the cup down. "You're brave to do this. I have a daughter almost your age—Ali. I can imagine how you must feel." She sighed and looked down at her cup.

"Mom and Dad are working things out," Jan said. "And they will, too," she added hastily. "They are doing great now."

"That's why you came?" Allyson spoke gently. "Because they were doing great?"

Jan looked down at her glass of Coke. She jiggled the ice around with the straw. "I just wanted it to be over," she murmured. "I just wanted them to go back to the way they used to be."

"Well, I understand that. But, Jan, they have to work it out themselves. There's nothing I can do . . . or you, either." Allyson leaned forward and patted Jan's hand. "You're looking in the wrong place. The answer to their problems is with them."

Jan expected to flinch from Allyson's touch, but she didn't. "I guess it was dumb to come," she said.

"No. It shows you care. It took guts to come down here and look for me. You want me to be the answer. But it doesn't work that way. Nobody's life is that neat, Jan. Your dad and I shouldn't have done what we did, but I can't tell you we didn't care about each other, that it didn't happen."

"He really loves my mom," Jan said. "And me and Josh."

"Oh, Jan, what's *really?* Have you thought about that? Don't people have a lot of feelings, all at the same time? Don't you love your mom and dad and hate them sometimes, too? Aren't both feelings real?"

Jan's thoughts went back to the train ride, to the way her window had gone by first one kind of world and then another, all baking under the same July sun. "People have to have real, true feelings," she said. "Just sometimes they forget them."

"Your dad loves your mom and you and your brother. But he has other feelings, too, and they're all real and true. Life isn't like a story that gets all tied up in a bow at the end. It's not neat. Life is a muddle, Jan."

"That's terrible." Jan's eyes widened. "Mom means everything to my dad. I know that, underneath, they've always loved each other."

"Your dad wants to stick with his family. He loves all of you. There's nothing you can do but wait while he and your mom try to work it out."

Jan finished her Coke. She crumpled her paper napkin and mopped her lips, then put it down on the table. She couldn't think what else to say. "I have to catch my bus." Jan pulled the strap of her purse over her shoulder. "It was nice meeting you," she added automatically. Then she thought how dumb that sounded and crunched her ice up and down with the straw.

"I liked meeting you," Allyson said. "It's easy to see why Ken's so proud of you." She stood up and held her hand out. Jan thought Allyson was going to pat her on the shoulder, but she was offering to shake hands. Like adults. Jan shook Allyson's hand, then reached for her wallet.

"I'll take care of it," Allyson said. "You go ahead."

Outside, the sun baked down and the smell of roasting pretzels and grilling hot dogs floated past. Jan didn't feel the heat, smell the food, or hear the city noises all around her. She was enclosed in her own in-sulated space. Everything had turned upside down. Nothing was the way she thought. A homeless woman almost pushed her shopping cart over her toes as Jan stepped blindly in her path. Jan found a spot on the bench inside the bus shelter and sat down. When the bus came, she climbed on and settled into her seat with a sigh. Jan leaned her face against the window glass, needing the coolness. At the train station, she got out and went in to buy her ticket.

On the train, Jan kept looking out the window at the city streets below the train tracks. "Life is a muddle," she said hesitantly to herself. Well, it certainly *looked* like a muddle. All around her, cars jerked forward and stopped; people sat on their front steps, talking and laughing. Little kids and old people and teenagers. Homeless people and policemen and guys fixing the street. High overhead, a man in a hard hat balanced on a steel beam, working on a new office tower. The city buzzed and boomed outside her window.

Jan watched a young Hispanic woman pushing a baby stroller with twins. The train pulled past and left them behind. At the edge of the city, they went past blocks of brick apartments. In one, the windows were open and Jan could see right in, to a kitchen table pushed against the curtains. A loaf of bread was sitting on the table. A gray cat poked its head out and yawned. The train gathered speed, leaving the city behind. It began snaking past the tall fences and cedar hedges that hid suburban houses from prying eyes.

Jan turned away from the window. She closed her eyes and heard Allyson's voice, saw Allyson's pale eyes looking kindly into hers. She liked Allyson. Was that *awful?* It had to be awful. The woman who had made her mom so miserable. Who had close to wrecked her parents' marriage. How could she be so *nice?* Was it really Allyson's fault that her mom and dad had problems? But if it wasn't, what were their problems? What made her dad care about Allyson? Jan was dizzy. She opened her eyes and focused on the back of the orange-patterned seat in front of her. An endless chain of questions trailed into her mind one after the other like the cars of the train, as the wheels slid along the tracks, taking her back to Forest Grove.

Two days after Jan's trip, her mom came home at noon and dropped her car keys onto the kitchen table with a jangle. The hospital wouldn't keep Gram anymore. They were sending her back to the nursing home. "She's stable now," Karen said, her voice catching. "They say it's just custodial care she needs. She'll go to the acute care section at Mapleview. I'll have to sort through her things and pack them up. In acute care, she'll just have a bed in a ward."

"You shouldn't have to do that by yourself. I'll take the afternoon off," Ken said.

"Let Josh and me help, too," Jan said. "I think we all ought to be there."

"Sure," Josh said. "I'll get some boxes out of the basement. And I'll help pack like I did when we moved."

The ambulance was bringing Gram at four. The McIvers went to the nursing home at three to clean out her old room and to be there when they wheeled Gram in. Jan packed the photographs that Gram had sitting on her bureau and along her window shelf . . . family pictures, all familiar to Jan . . . pictures of her and Josh from when they were babies, of Mom before she was married, and one of Mom and Dad at their wedding. Pictures of Jan's granddad when he was young and had dark hair and a mustache, and of Gram with her hair cut short and permed in smooth waves around her ears. Gram's mouth was a bow with dark lipstick and her eyes sparkled with mischief. Jan had seen the picture hundreds of times, but now she paused over it. Where was that girl now? Was she still there somewhere, inside Gram?

Wrapping the pictures, looking at them closely for the first time, Jan was reminded again of her trip into the city. It was as if each person in the family wasn't just one person, but a parade of them, all side by side in frames on Gram's shelf. Even herself. A tiny baby, a chubby toddler, a serious eight-year-old with braids. The same, but different. Jan was beginning to think she'd never get at the truth behind any of it, never even settle on exactly who she was herself, because tomorrow she might be changing into somebody else. She wrapped each picture in newspaper and nested them in a cardboard box.

Her mom was taking Gram's clothes out of the closet and bureau drawers. Josh and her dad were unhooking the TV and VCR. Jan saw her mom blinking back tears and went to help her with the clothes.

"I'm glad all of you came," her mom said in a choked voice. "It's a time when family counts."

"Hold that box steady, Josh, while I lower the TV in," her dad said.

Jan leaned on the bureau for a minute, remembering Gram's party . . . her dad had bumbled with the
wrappings and ribbons and her mom had rattled on,
being cheerful. Jan had kept wishing that somebody
would do or say just the right thing, and she'd strained
and strained to figure out what that was. Now she wondered if there was a "right thing."

The four of them piled the boxes on the bed and
got ready to carry them out to the car.

"Is that everything?" Jan's mom moved close beside Jan's dad, their shoulders almost touching, as she
took a last look around.

"I'll take these boxes out," Ken said. "Then we
could wait in the lounge to see Lucille settled in."

"The ambulance ought to be here in a few minutes." Karen checked her watch.

"Afterward, could we go get hamburgers?" Josh
asked. "I want a double cheeseburger."

"Sure," Karen said. "We'll go to the Burger Factory.
How'll that be?"

"Awesome! Can I have a shake, too?"

From the lounge window Jan saw the ambulance
pull into the curved drive out front. Two men got out,

opened up the doors, and wheeled Gram in. Gram's hands quivered, weaving a restless pattern in the air, like someone knitting with no yarn.

They all followed the men pushing the stretcher down the hall. Gram's bed was in a row with others; most of the patients were hooked to some kind of plastic tubing. The woman in the bed next to where they put Gram was picking at her tube and muttering in a low voice that was almost a kind of song. Jan winced, seeing the men about to lift Gram, but they barely disturbed her.

"Ready? One, two, three," the guy at the head said, and they swung her onto the mattress by lifting her on the sheet under her body. Then they rolled her onto her side and pulled it out. Gram didn't change expression. Once she was on her back again, her eyes wandered across the ceiling. Karen took her hand and stroked her arm.

"Mom? You're back," she said. "At Mapleview. That's nice, isn't it? No more hospital." They stood around the bed and listened to Gram breathe in hoarse little gasps.

"It's hard on them, the transition," the nurse who'd

followed them in said. "I'll give her a sedative, calm her down. She'll sleep the rest of the afternoon."

Jan's dad touched her mom's elbow. "Karen," he said gently. "Karen, we should leave now. Let Lucille rest."

Jan's mom blinked, as if she were waking up from a dream. She'd been staring at her mom's face. "You're right," she said. She let go of Gram's hand and laid it down next to her body on top of the sheet. The McIvers turned away from the bed and walked to the door. Jan looked back for one more glimpse of Gram before the door swung shut. Gram was still staring at the ceiling.

It was early to eat . . . only five. Even so, Jan was starved. All the way to the Burger Factory, she pictured the meat, the melted cheddar cheese, and the browned onions she wanted on top. She toyed with having tomato and lettuce, but rejected the idea. She wanted the meat juice to flood her mouth, the sweet grilled onions to rest on her tongue.

In the booth, the four of them waited for their food without saying much. Jan caught her dad looking longingly at the pile of newspapers that were there for customers to read, but he didn't get one. He jiggled his fork. Was he thinking about Allyson? Did he wish he was with her? Jan looked down at her place mat and read the map of Burger Factory locations.

"Can I have some quarters? For the video games?" Josh was off in a flash to the video corridor by the entrance. Jan and her mom excused themselves and went to the ladies' room.

"Funny," her mom said, pressing the faucet button to wash her hands. "I mean, you wouldn't think I'd want to eat for hours, not after all that. But to tell you the truth, I'm starved."

"Same here," Jan said, hitting the knob to turn on the hot-air dryer and sticking her hands under it. Jan wiped the last dampness off her hands onto her T- shirt, her mom fluttered her fingers under the gush of hot wind, and then they walked together back to the booth. The waitress had brought their burgers. Her dad had ordered a big basket of curly fries to share. Jan ran to fetch Josh and they all dug in.

"Crispy," her mom said, dipping a potato curl in ketchup. "Good. Even if you wouldn't want to eat them every day."

"Yum," Josh said. *"I'd* eat them every day."

"Thinking about a career," Ken said to Josh, "you might as well cross off dietician."

"Or chef, for that matter." Karen laughed. "You'll never be another Galloping Gourmet."

"He'll make millions," Jan said. "Designing ways to zap people on video screens." She took a big bite of her burger. It was done just right, still juicy. Chewing, she glanced around at the four of them. Her mom was holding her bun gingerly and leaning forward over her plate, careful with her drips. Her dad had already chomped away half of his burger. Josh had opened his bun to scrape off the pickles. He passed them over to her automatically—Jan loved pickles; Josh hated them.

"Thanks," she said, putting a sweet slice into her mouth. The four of them ate quietly. A line from *LBA* hovered in her mind as they all sat there together: "What is there, in the end, but family and friends?" She thought it, but she didn't say it. "They really do make great hamburgers here," she said instead.